WHO STOLE THE HAMSTER?

N. GRIFFIN

illustrated by
KATE HINDLEY

**WALKER
BOOKS**

So many people were kind enough to read and comment and listen to me babble around about this book! For all that I'd like to thank Tobin, Jane G-K, Allen K., Kelley L., Darsa M., Kathi A., my sister, her husband, and my niece.

I'd especially like to thank Karen Lotz and everyone at Candlewick who have been so wonderful about making Smashie into a book. You are just the best!

First published in Great Britain 2017 by Walker Books Ltd
87 Vauxhall Walk, London SE11 5HJ

2 4 6 8 10 9 7 5 3

Text © 2015 by N. Griffin
Illustration © 2015 by Kate Hindley

The right of N. Griffin and Kate Hindley to be identified as author and illustrator respectively of this work has been asserted by them in accordance with the Copyright, Designs and Patents Act 1988

This book has been typeset in Dante

Printed and bound in Great Britain by Clays Ltd

British Library Cataloguing in Publication Data:
a catalogue record for this book is available from the British Library

ISBN 978-1-4063-7456-8

www.walker.co.uk

For E and E!

N. G.

To Arlo, Carrie, and Hal

K. H.

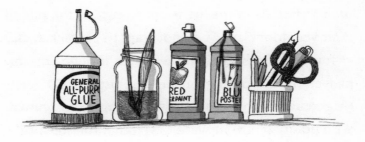

CHAPTER 1

The Archenemy

The day Patches was stolen from Smashie McPepper's class started out like any other day. Well, except for the fact that her teacher was out sick and Smashie's class was stuck with the worst substitute in the world. And except for the mysterious business with the glue. And except for the fact that Patches himself had become Smashie's new archenemy.

"I do not want to go back to Room 11," said Smashie to her best friend, Dontel Marquise. Art was just ending, and the two of them were cleaning up their materials in the art room alongside the rest of their year four class. "I do not want to go back at all."

It wasn't just because art was over, though Smashie had enjoyed working on her Prehistoric 3D scene (frightened prehistoric people fleeing from animals with pointy teeth). It wasn't even that the substitute, Mr Carper, was lying in wait for them back in the classroom. Smashie's reason for not wanting to return was both smaller and larger than either of those things.

"Don't worry, Smash," said Dontel, putting away his own model (thoughtful prehistoric people working out how to invent tools). "It'll get easier. You'll get used to it."

Smashie shook her head. "No," she said. "I will never get used to it."

Feet dragging, she attached herself to the end of the line of her classmates gathered at the art room door.

"What if you make one of your suits?" Dontel asked, coming up beside her. "You could make a Brave Suit to wear in Room 11."

"I do not need a Brave Suit!" Smashie cried. "I am

not unbrave about what's in our room! I just think it is awful."

"Hrrm," said Dontel.

Perhaps Dontel was right, though, Smashie thought. Perhaps a suit would help. She was only just wearing regular dungarees today, but she often wore suits of her own devising. When she and Dontel had participated in the year three maths competition last year, for example, she had made a Maths Suit by painting numbers on an old opera cape of her grandma's and pasting equations to the toes of her wellies. And when she had rashly signed up to man the present-wrapping table at the Mother's Day fair last spring, her Present-Wrapping Suit had been the only thing that had gotten her through the day. (Smashie was not at her best with a pair of scissors. Cutting things always led to plasters and a trip to the school nurse, and the present wrapping had been no exception. Nonetheless, in her suit, she had persevered.)

At various other times, Smashie had created Writing Suits, Cooking Suits, and Distracting-Adults-from-Messes Suits. Being in a suit always helped

Smashie get into the right frame of mind to solve hard problems.

"I can't think of a suit that could help me with this problem," Smashie said now as she and Dontel and the rest of their class arrived at Room 11. "Room 11 is wrecked forever."

"Smashie," said Dontel, "it is only a hamster."

Patches.

It was his feet that got her. The rest of the hamster's body was all right, Smashie supposed: round with tan fur and nervous black eyes. But his feet!

"A little soft creature should have little soft feet!" Smashie had cried to Dontel when the rest of the class decided that a hamster would be the perfect class pet after a series of strenuous discussions the previous week. "But Patches has claws! Terrible, scrabbly claws!"

"Now, Smashie," Dontel had said soothingly, "I think you just don't really understand about hamsters. There are reasons they have that kind of feet. Hamsters are—"

"They are two kinds of creature, smushed together; that's what they are. It's like somebody stuck a chicken's feet onto a mouse's body! What kind of creature is two kinds of creature?"

Dontel thought for a moment. "What about the sphinx?" he'd offered at last. "You liked learning about the sphinx during our ancient Egypt project. And Asten, the dog-headed, ape-bodied servant of the god Thoth – you loved him, too."

"Hamsters are nothing like dog-headed, ape-bodied Asten! Asten is wonderful." Smashie shuddered and raked her hands through her hair. "Hamsters look like a crazy biologist bashed different animals together to make a monster!"

"Smashie…"

"Like that guy Dr Frankenstein made! *Our class is*

getting a Frankenstein rodent monster!" Dontel patted her shoulder, but Smashie shook his hand off. She was very worked up. Even Dontel could not calm her.

Smashie herself had argued for a lizard. "It would be like having a miniature dinosaur! It would fit perfectly with our project on prehistoric times, Ms Early!"

"We are not studying pre-*human* times, Smashie," Ms Early had said. "Just prehistoric."

But Smashie pressed on. "At least lizards are *uniform*. And most lizards are vegetarians, too!"

She thought the last point would go over well with the children who had been opposed to Billy Kamarski's suggestion of a mouse-eating snake.

But no. The rest of the class was firm. They wanted a hamster. So Patches had been selected and purchased and brought to their room just yesterday. And because his cage was right next to the children's coat area, there had been plenty of opportunities for Smashie to confront the reality of his feet.

Like right now, for example. Caught in the throng of students heading to the back of the room, Smashie was forced to stop in front of Patches's cage as the children came to a halt to admire him.

"Look how sweet he is," said Jacinda Morales.

"I *know*," moaned Charlene Stott. "He is the cutest darling boy!"

Smashie gulped.

"Come on, Smash," whispered Dontel encouragingly. "Don't you think he is at least a little bit cute?"

Patches trembled on his bed of wooden shavings.

"No," said Smashie, and gulped again.

What if Patches manages somehow to open the door to his cage and escape? she thought hectically. What if he made his way to her seat and crawled on her with those awful feet?

"Do you think Patches would ever be able to open that cage?" she asked Dontel, her brow creased with worry.

Dontel sighed. "No," he said. "I don't. He would need thumbs to work the latch."

"Phew," said Smashie.

In front of them, Willette Williams poked her forefinger through the bars of the cage to stroke Patches's head. "I hate that he had to spend his first night here in the classroom all alone," she mourned.

"He was fine," said Billy Kamarski gruffly. "Patches is tough."

Smashie and Dontel exchanged surprised glances. It was not like Billy to have a soft spot for a hamster. Mostly what Billy liked was playing jokes on his class-mates. Last week, for example, he had telephoned Smashie.

"Is your refrigerator running?" he asked.

"Yes," Smashie answered.

"Then you'd better go catch it!" he yelled, and hung up, laughing insanely.

"That joke is as old as Methuselah," Smashie's grandmother had said. Both Smashie and Dontel had grandmothers who lived with them and kept an eye on them after school. The two grandmothers were close friends and saw eye to eye on the subject of Smashie and Dontel.

Jokes like Billy's refrigerator joke were irritating, but some of his jokes were downright unkind. He was always giving people wedgies, for example. And once he put a plastic tarantula in Siggie Higgins's work box, when everybody knew that Siggie was truly frightened of spiders. Smashie had kindly fished it out of the box for him while Dontel calmed Siggie down and reassured him that it wasn't real. Billy, on the other hand, had collapsed on the floor and drummed his heels with mirth.

Getting in trouble never seemed to deter Billy from his pranks, either. He got into plenty for the wedgies and the tarantula in Siggie's box, but that didn't stop him from laughing like a loon at the very mention of a spider.

But now even Billy was being extra nice to the hamster.

Patches squirmed and wriggled and scratched on his shavings. Then he grasped Willette's finger tightly in his forepaws.

"Oh!" Willette cried, and swooned with joy.

Smashie swooned with horror. She rounded on Dontel, who shook his head warningly.

"Don't say you think hamsters look like a zoo-logical experiment gone wrong," he whispered. "Don't, Smashie. The kids got really mad when you said that last week."

Smashie subsided.

"You are right," she said. "And a lot of them are still mad at me, too."

This was the other part of Smashie's problem. Although she was generally well liked in Room 11, the pet debate had gotten rather sticky in the end. And Smashie had not made things any better yesterday when they had voted on the hamster's name.

"He doesn't even *have* patches!" she'd complained.

But none of the other children would consent to name him, as Smashie had suggested, Uggles de Blucky. And they had not been shy about expressing their feelings about her suggestion.

"You are being mean, Smashie McPepper!" Joyce Costa had cried.

"How can you say such awful things about the animal we love?" Willette had agreed with accusing eyes.

Standing amid her happy classmates now, Smashie had to admit it was lonely being the only member of Room 11 who did not love Patches. Even Dontel liked him. He liked him a lot. It was one of the few times that Smashie's and Dontel's minds were not as one.

Mostly, Smashie and Dontel had so much in common that they were practically twins. Besides having grandmas at home, they both enjoyed cartoons with a lot of action and milk shakes with extra ice cream. They were co-champions of last year's maths competition, and they'd won the lower-school spelling competition as well. And both of them loved to think about complicated things. As with the hamster, Smashie's thoughts tended to be hectic and shouty, while Dontel's were calm and well constructed. But when they put their two kinds of thinking together, Smashie and Dontel were an unstoppable team.

So the fact that Dontel did not mind the purchase of Patches – was even happy about it – threw Smashie.

Maybe I am wrong, Smashie thought now. *Maybe Patches is secretly cool.*

She stared at the little rodent. If he was secretly cool, it was a very big secret.

Maybe if I think of him as Patches as in eye patches, she thought. *Like a pirate.* She imagined a little circle of black fabric cocked rakishly over one of Patches's eyes and pictured him striding fearlessly about in his cage, as if on the deck of a ship.

But the real Patches did not swashbuckle. He quivered. And scratched again.

Smashie sighed.

Maybe if I imagine him with a cutlass and peg leg, too, she thought. And a less trembly personality.

But Smashie was interrupted in her thinking by an irritated voice barking at them from the front of the room.

"Kids!" the voice boomed. "Stop mooning over that animal and sit down."

It was Mr Carper. The substitute.

CHAPTER 2
The Substitute

The children slumped and turned.

Smashie felt bad for Ms Early because she was out with the stomach flu, but she felt worse for Room 11. Ms Early, at least, did not have to spend the day under the care of Mr Carper.

Mr Carper was convinced that his discovery as a fashion model was imminent. "Mother always says I'm the handsomest man in any room," he was wont to say. "And it's my aim to share that with the world." Indeed, a close-up of his teeth had once been featured in an ad for the town dentist, and ever since he had refused to take a full-time job, working only as a substitute at the Rebecca Lee Crumpler Primary School so that he would be available when his big moment came.

"Children," Mr Carper said now, his eyes following his every move in his reflection in the classroom door, "sit down. And zip your lips." He adjusted his collar, tossed his head in a manner suggestive of more hair than was currently attached to his head, and tugged down his jumper a careful few centimetres.

Normally Smashie would have been very happy to be taught by someone who put so much thought into what he was wearing. But Mr Carper's outfits did not seem to help him concentrate the way Smashie's suits did. Instead, they seemed to take his attention quite away from things he should be paying attention to. Like teaching.

Smashie and Dontel exchanged a speaking look and headed to their seats with the rest of the class.

"Not a word from anyone until I've read the morning announcements," said Mr Carper. "And not even then, unless I say so."

Usually Ms Early read out the announcements first thing, but the children had barely hung up their coats this morning before Mr Carper had hustled them out of the classroom for art. He took up the paper now, but, eyes still fixed on his reflection in the door, turned his head briefly from side to side before settling on a view of himself from the right. He leaned back on Ms Early's desk and began to read:

"THE REBECCA LEE CRUMPLER PRIMARY SCHOOL

PENELOPE ARMSTRONG, HEADMISTRESS

MORNING ANNOUNCEMENTS

TUESDAY, OCTOBER 3

Good morning, Rebecca Lee Crumpler students.

ANNOUNCEMENT 1: An exciting day for RLC year sixes today! Mr Bloom, the school caretaker, will give a guest lecture in their class at noon on the topic 'Astronomy – Now and for the Future.'"

"I'd like to hear that," whispered Dontel, who planned to be an astronomer when he grew up. One of his most cherished possessions was an

autographed copy of Neil deGrasse Tyson's *The Sky Is Not the Limit: Adventures of an Urban Astrophysicist.*

"Me too," said Smashie. "We could find out how to fire a rocket."

Mr Carper continued reading:

"ANNOUNCEMENT 2: Miss Dismont's class is away for the day at the Natural History Museum. We hope they enjoy their work in the exhibit of rare minerals and gems. ANNOUNCEMENT 3: Tomorrow, all students will attend a special assembly about the importance of good nutrition, sponsored by Mrs True, owner of the TrueYum supermarket."

"The TrueYum, eh? How about that." Mr Carper lowered the paper and looked meaningfully at the students. "I'm sure you kids have heard about The Search."

"What search?" asked Cyrus Hull.

"'*What search?*' Boy with Glasses, do you live under a rock?"

"No," said Cyrus.

"I probably shouldn't tell you," said Mr Carper.

"But who cares? You're a homely bunch, so you're no real competition." He leaned back and smirked at the class. "I have it on good authority," he said, "that Mrs True is looking for someone to model for the TrueYum's upcoming supermarket circular. And you know I don't like to mention this, because I don't want to be treated differently from any other substitute, but I do have modeling experience."

"We know," said Charlene wearily.

"The dentist ad," said John Singletary.

"You've told us," said Jacinda. "More than once."

"Don't be embarrassed, Long-Haired Girl," Mr Carper said with a laugh. "Lots of people recognize me."

"From substituting?" asked Willette.

"No, Girl in Plaid," snapped Mr Carper, his laughter switched off like a tap. "From *these*." And he flashed his teeth at the class.

"Mr Carper," said Dontel, "it's nine forty-five. We're supposed to do science now."

But Mr Carper wasn't listening. He picked up a plastic apple from Ms Early's desk and held it against his cheek, gazing coyly at them. They regarded him silently. Mr Carper put the apple back down.

"No," he muttered. "I need to practice with the big stuff. A watermelon, maybe. Some kind of meat." He drew himself to his feet. "There's something else in my favour," he said. "I have reason to believe – and you'll all understand this – that Mrs True ... admires me."

"Uck," whispered Jacinda.

"She's a widow, you know. And just the other week, I was in the groceries section at the TrueYum, squeezing cantaloupes, when she sailed up beside me. 'With that jawline, Marlon,' she said—"

"Bleh," muttered Alonso Day.

"So one might say," said Mr Carper, "that I am something of a front-runner to land the modeling job for that circular." His eyes narrowed as he glanced again at the page of announcements and continued to read:

"The assembly will start promptly at one o'clock tomorrow in the school hall."

Mr Carper tapped his teeth with a pen. "Will Mrs True be there, I wonder?"

"Sure," said Siggie. "She comes every year."

"What, Boy with the Weird Trousers? Did you say yes, she'll be there?" Mr Carper began a slow, measured walk around the room.

Siggie hesitated, and glanced at his trousers. "Um, I think so?" he said.

"Of course she'll be there," said Jacinda. "She's one of the town's leading citizens."

"Now, that," said Mr Carper, "is of interest." His lip curled as he passed by Patches's cage. "Disgusting," he said.

"What!" squawked Cyrus.

"Hamsters," said Mr Carper. "Totally gross. They spend the day sitting around in their own filth." He shuddered. "I can't stand them."

The class stirred angrily.

Smashie drew in her breath sharply.

It was awful but true. Despite his rude personal comments and stance against interesting school-work, Smashie felt a deep kinship with Mr Carper.

Little did she know that their shared hatred would come back to haunt her after Patches had been stolen.

"All right, let me finish reading the rest of this nonsense." Mr Carper's eyes slid down the page of morning announcements as he paced and continued to read: "'We know all our students are in for a fine day of learning...' Blah and blah... 'Think hard and work well...'"

Mr Carper crumpled the paper. "Okay, whatever, that's enough."

Charlene furrowed her brow. "Does it really say *blah and blah*, Mr Carper?"

"Oh, Girl with the Shirt." Mr Carper glanced at the clock. "Hope that you grow up beautiful."

Charlene's outraged gasp was drowned out by a crash as the door of Room 11 flew open. In its frame stood Mrs Armstrong, headmistress of the Rebecca Lee Crumpler Primary School.

CHAPTER 3
The Prank

"Mr Carper!" boomed Mrs Armstrong, twin snorts of air puffing through her nostrils and her eyes practically on fire.

Mr Carper wheeled around and put a friendly hand on Charlene's shoulder. Charlene shrugged it furiously off.

"Why, hello, Mrs Armstrong!" said Mr Carper, making his voice extra deep. He smiled winningly at the principal.

"I am *ill*, Mr Carper," cried the headmistress. "I am SIMPLY ILL!"

"I misspoke, Mrs Armstrong," said Mr Carper, his smile rather strained. "I'm sure she'll grow up to be a real stunner—"

The headmistress looked at Mr Carper with furrowed brows. "What are you talking about?"

"Are you ill with the flu, Mrs Armstrong?" Smashie asked anxiously.

"No." Mrs Armstrong swept her eyes toward Smashie. "I am not. Though it is very kind of you to ask, Smashie. What I meant, children—" she raised her voice—"is that I am SIMPLY ILL ABOUT THE BEHAVIOUR OF ROOM 11!"

Mr Carper sagged. "Thank goodness."

Mrs Armstrong eyed him with distaste.

"I mean," said Mr Carper hastily, "how awful that my little charges have misbehaved."

"Mr Carper," said Mrs Armstrong tersely, "this has nothing to do with you."

"Great," said Mr Carper.

Mrs Armstrong raised her brows at him briefly before turning her glower to the class. "But it has everything to do with you, Room 11. I am heartily disappointed!"

"What did we do?" cried Jacinda.

"THIS!" Mrs Armstrong stepped into the room and flung her hand dramatically toward the door. "Enter, Mr Flake!"

Mr Flake, the art teacher, stepped reluctantly into the room. He stood before the class, his large moustache drooping over his mouth.

"Your hand!" Mrs Armstrong commanded.

Silently, Mr Flake held up his left hand, the fingers of which were curled over a ruler. Slowly, he unfurled them. Astonishingly, the ruler did not fall to the ground but remained stuck straight across the palm of his hand.

"Magic," breathed Smashie.

"No." Dontel shook his head. "Glue."

He was right.

"Who glued Mr Flake's hand to this ruler, Room 11?" thundered Mrs Armstrong.

Nobody answered.

Smashie's and Dontel's eyes met. Plastic tarantulas, rude phone calls – who else would glue a teacher to a ruler? Dollars to doughnuts, it was Billy Kamarski.

They were not alone in their thinking. All eyes had turned to Billy.

"Hey!" shouted Billy, looking from child to child. "What are you all looking at me for?"

"Mr Kamarski?" Mrs Armstrong said sternly. "Have you something to say?"

"Heck no!" Billy cried. "It wasn't me!"

Siggie snorted.

"Like heck it wasn't," muttered John Singletary.

"Who, then?" Mrs Armstrong trumpeted. "This class was the last to have art. You were the last to use the rulers. Nobody else has entered or exited the art room this morning!"

Smashie and Dontel did not believe in pointing fingers, but they did believe firmly in people taking responsibility. Smashie drew together her brows and glared in Billy's direction. Dontel fixed him with a very stern look.

The students were silent.

Finally, someone whispered, "Come on, Billy."

Billy's head whipped round. "I told you, it wasn't me!"

The children stared at him accusingly.

Mrs Armstrong waited.

Silence.

"Fine!" she said. "Come along! Immediately! All of you!"

"All of us?" cried Smashie. "Do you think *all of us* glued Mr Flake to a ruler, Mrs Armstrong?"

"Certainly I do not," said Mrs Armstrong. "But I believe *one* of you did, and until that person comes forward, you will all spend from now until the end of morning break – a silent morning break, Room 11 – with me. In my office."

"But, Mrs Armstrong, that's not fair!" cried John.

"Neither is gluing people to things!" Mrs Armstrong cried. "Isn't that right, Mr Flake?"

Mr Flake looked gloomily at his hand and nodded.

"Punishing them sounds like a good idea, Mrs Armstrong," Mr Carper said.

John shook his head in disgust.

"I'll just wait for them here," Mr Carper continued. "More practice time for me." He cast an eye over the stacks on Ms Early's desk. "There's got to be something I can pose with around here. Every teacher has a secret stash of granola bars or something lying around, right?"

Mrs Armstrong eyed him distastefully.

"Our staff takes its snacks in the staffroom, Mr Carper," she said. "Feel free to join them if you wish." She turned back to the children. "Form a line, Room 11. File!"

"Mr Carper is happy that we're in trouble!" whispered Smashie to Dontel as the class headed down the hall.

"I think he's just happy to be rid of us," Dontel whispered back.

They were not the only ones talking out of turn. The line of children fairly hissed with upset speech as it filed past Miss Dismont's empty classroom next door.

"I wish *we* were at the Natural History Museum, like Miss Dismont's class."

"Me too!"

"That Billy—"

"If we have to miss break because of him—"

Willette stopped short just ahead of Smashie. "Who will take care of

Patches while we're gone?" she cried.

"Patches will be fine, Willette," Dontel reassured her.

"We will only be out of the room for fifteen minutes," said Smashie.

"But he'll be all alone! With Mr Carper, who hates him! You might not care if Patches is happy, Smashie McPepper," she cried, eyes narrowing, "but the rest of us do!"

Better Patches in there with Mr Carper than us, thought Smashie. Aloud, however, she said only, "I never said I wanted Patches to be unhappy, Willette!"

But Willette was inconsolable. "Oh, Patches!" she cried.

Smashie and Dontel exchanged looks. Willette, they agreed, loved Patches almost Too Much.

They filed into Mrs Armstrong's office.

CHAPTER 4

On Punishment

It was awful. The children were cramped together in tight rows on the floor. Mrs Armstrong glowered over them.

"It wasn't me!" Billy cried for the thousandth time.

"Sure, it wasn't, Billy," said John.

"Why do you always think things are my fault?"

"Because they always are!" Jacinda shouted back.

"We must not accuse others unfairly, Room 11," said Mrs Armstrong. "Did anyone see Billy perform this terrible act?"

The children looked at one another. Nobody had.

"See?" cried Billy. "You're just blaming me because I have an awful reputation."

"And because you were supplies monitor in art today," Smashie muttered darkly to Dontel.

The conversation only deteriorated from there.

"Enough!" Mrs Armstrong said. "If no one will take responsibility, Room 11 must continue to be punished as a body. You will have silent morning breaks in your room each day. And lunchtime privileges will be closed to you until further notice as well. You will be permitted to talk quietly amongst yourselves at the rear of the playground, but athletics – playing on the swings and climbing on the play structure – will be quite off-limits." She stood up. "That is all. You may go."

The children squabbled their way back to their classroom.

"The whole class is being punished, and it's all because of you, Billy!" cried Joyce.

"I was looking forward to a good game of flag football today," said Cyrus. "And now – nothing!"

"Nothing," echoed Dontel, shaking his head.

Although he and Smashie often played together at breaktime, when Dontel played sports, Smashie did not join him. Mostly because she was the sort of person who forgot to pay attention to the game and got clonked on the head with the ball.

"This puts me in a mood, Kamarski," said John.

"I didn't do it!" Billy shouted again.

"Sure, kid. Tell us another one," said Cyrus, one eyebrow raised.

"But it *wasn't me!*" Billy cried as they reached the classroom door.

"Why can't he just admit it?" said Smashie. "Poor Mr Flake."

"Well," said Dontel, "maybe it wasn't him."

"Tchah," said Smashie, and pushed open the door to Room 11.

Mr Carper, standing at the back of the room by the coat area and Patches's cage, leaped up as if stung.

"What are you doing back here?" he cried.

"It's our classroom, Mr Carper," Dontel explained. "We're supposed to come here to learn things."

"Learn things," muttered Mr Carper. "Sweet mercy."

He straightened up.

"I hope that talking-to made you all feel bad," he said. "Things are going to be a lot tighter in here from now on."

"Tighter!" said Smashie to Dontel. "How could they get any tighter?"

"Sit," said Mr Carper. "Now."

As he spoke, his eyes were fixed on the front of the room, and he tossed his head up, then down, then to the side.

"What is he doing?" Dontel whispered as the children headed to their spots.

Smashie craned her neck. "I think he is trying to catch sight of himself in the mirror on the top of the overhead projector."

"Quiet, Girl with the Ears!"

What!

"Who does he think he is!" Smashie whispered furiously, grasping her ears. "Sub with the Meanness, is who! Why, I ought to—" She took a deep breath. Mr Carper might be in a bad temper, but that was nothing compared to what he would be once she started shouting.

But Mr Carper was already talking again.

"First of all," he said, "none of you is to come near this hamster for the rest of the day. It's closed to you."

"Closed to us!" cried Willette.

"But, Mr Carper!" cried Charlene. "We have to feed him and give him water!"

"I already fed the awful thing," said Mr Carper.

"Thing!" squawked Billy just as Siggie, whose day it was to feed Patches, emitted an outraged yelp.

"And it has plenty of water." Mr Carper threw a

baleful look over his shoulder at the little rodent. "So stay clear."

"But why? Are *you* punishing us, too?"

Mr Carper pushed himself away from the cage. "Yes," he said. "And also because those things carry germs like crazy and this school is already full of people with the flu. I'm not about to increase my chances of getting sick, not with the circular gig on the line. So stay away from that rodent," he said. "And from me, too. As much as possible."

"Mr Carper hates Patches as much as he hates us," Willette whispered to her tablemates.

"No kidding," said Charlene. "What kind of awful person wouldn't love Patches?"

"Hmm," said Joyce, and turned and frowned under her heavy fringe in Smashie's direction. The two other girls followed her gaze and shook their heads, lips pursed.

Smashie broke off thinking vengeful thoughts about Mr Carper and stared at her knees. Her shoulder blades scrunched uncomfortably. Dontel looked hard in the other direction.

Scrabble, scrabble, scrabble, went Patches in the back of the room.

How could Smashie have known that those were some of the last *scrabble, scrabble* noises that Room 11 would hear from Patches that day? How could she have known that in just a couple of hours, Patches would go missing and that she herself would be the person most concerned with his recovery?

CHAPTER 5

Thwarted

"Ten thirty," Mr Carper moaned, glancing at the clock. "What am I going to do with you until lunch?"

"We should do what we missed this morning." Dontel got up and moved to the back of the room. "I'll get the aluminum foil we need for our science projects."

"I'll pass out the directions," said Jacinda, hopping up to join him.

"I'll pour out the black paint," said Smashie.

"Hey," said Mr Carper. "'Who said you could just get up and mill around?"

"We're getting ready for science," said Smashie.

"*Science,*" said Mr Carper as if Smashie had suggested the class have a go at pole-vaulting. "What do you mean, *science*?" He glanced at the packet of lesson plans Ms Early had left.

"We've been studying light in science for weeks, Mr Carper," said Alonso. "Today we're supposed to make pinhole cameras."

"Whoa, whoa, whoa, whoa, *whoa,*" said Mr Carper, holding up his hand. "Whoa. No. Black paint? Spilly children? No way. I'd rather put a fork through my temples than deal with that combination." He crumpled Ms Early's plans in his hand.

"Only the painting part is messy, Mr Carper!" said Smashie. "And we wear big shirts over our regular shirts so we don't wreck them."

"Well, *I* don't wear big shirts over my regular shirts," said Mr Carper. "And I'm not risking any damage to this outfit."

"But, Mr Carper!"

"But nothing. It's called *school.* Not Pinhole

Camera Land. Where are those worksheet packets I made? Ah, here." He took up a stack of papers in his hand. "Sit down, Passing-Out-Stuff People. We're going to do these instead."

"But we brought in yogurt pots from home to make the cameras and everything!" Siggie gestured to the back of the room, where the pots lay in a large cardboard box near Patches's cage.

"I could pass those out as soon as I'm done with the aluminum foil," said Dontel.

"I SAID NO!"

The class jumped.

"Sit down."

Smashie and Dontel sat down. So did Jacinda.

"Grr," said Smashie.

"Hoo-boy," said Siggie. "Here we go."

"The man is in a temper," John agreed.

"What, Athletic-Looking Boy? Here, pass these out." Mr Carper dropped the stack of papers in front of John, who gave him the eye but rose from his seat.

Scowling, Smashie put down the paint containers beside her chair. All around her, the normal happy buzz of Room 11 was replaced by a grim silence as the children took out their pencils and started to work on Mr Carper's worksheets.

Smashie took up her own worksheet and read:

1. What is a food that rhymes with *wocolate*?

_____

She looked bleakly at Dontel, who shook his head in disgust.

"How does this count as *school*?" he said hopelessly.

But there was nothing for it. He and Smashie settled in to work.

"We better make these neat, too," said Dontel. "Or he'll make us rewrite them, just to waste time."

Smashie frowned. Her handwriting was terrible.

Mr Carper began to pace around the room, stopping in front of the maths materials to pick up one of the little mirrors Room 11 used when they worked on symmetry.

Mr Carper winked at himself. Then he made his face look friendly, yet knowing.

"Well, hello there, Mrs True," he murmured, passing a hand over his hair. Forming his fingers into the shape of a little gun, he winked at himself again and clicked it. Then he put down the mirror and continued around the room.

"Sharpen that pencil, Big Feet," said Mr Carper, absently twirling some keys on a chain around his neck as he passed John's desk.

"I thought I was Athletic-Looking Boy," said John.

"Don't be a baby – you're both. Slow down, Hair," he warned Alonso. "These sheets take some thought."

"Just take it, Singletary," John muttered to himself. "This is just one moment in the day."

"Mr Carper?" Alonso asked. "Why do you wear your keys around your neck? Why don't you just stick them in your pocket?"

"I never put anything in my pockets," said Mr Carper. "Mars the line of the clothes."

"Oh," said Alonso.

"Now, get to work."

Dontel's mouth fell open. "If he won't put anything in his pockets," he whispered to Smashie, "where does he put stuff he wants to think more about later?" Dontel's pockets were always stocked with items of this ilk. Like his astronomer idol, Dr Tyson, Dontel loved nothing more than figuring out how things worked and applying what he learned to new situations. So when he came across something that was potentially useful or interesting, it went right into his pocket to await further study or application. Right now, for example, he was carrying a miniature flashlight, a packet of mayonnaise, and a complex set of tiny interlocking parts from his family's old dishwasher, among other things. He'd figured out and explained to Smashie how the flashlight worked, as well as how to make mayonnaise, but was still figuring out the dishwasher parts.

"I don't imagine Mr Carper is all that interested

in thinking more about things later," Smashie muttered back.

Mr Carper walked on, whistling slightly. The whistling broke off.

"I'd like to give you a little something," he murmured.

"You would, Mr Carper?" asked Smashie, who was puzzled. "What do you want to give us?"

"What?" said Mr Carper, wheeling round. "I wasn't talking to you, Ears."

Smashie glowered. But Mr Carper wasn't paying any attention. He reached Ms Early's desk and sat down, settling in with a magazine.

An hour later, things were deteriorating in Room 11.

"What do you mean you can't list four brands of hair gel?" Mr Carper snarled at Charlene when she asked for help with question number six. "Don't you kids ever go shopping? Think! And, you back there – Kid in the Trainers – quit looking at that disgusting hamster!"

It went on and on until noon finally came and

Mr Carper led Smashie and the rest of her seething classmates to the canteen.

"I hate today," said Smashie as they reached the double doors.

"Me too," said Dontel. "What does the man have against thinking?"

"Could I go to the nurse, Mr Carper?" Billy Kamarski gulped. "I don't feel so good." He certainly was not looking tip-top.

"He's probably feeling terrible because of the scorn of his classmates," said Smashie.

"More likely that stomach flu that's going around," said Dontel. "Poor guy."

"*Poor guy*, nothing," said Jacinda firmly. "He's a big glue-pants."

"Yes, yes, go, Sick-Looking Kid," said Mr Carper. "Contain your germs. The rest of you – into the canteen. I swear," he said, turning and heading into the staffroom next door, "there are days when the only thing that gets me through is the thought of a glass of wine and two hours' research with a copy of *GQ*."

The door shut behind him.

CHAPTER 6

Anguish
on the
Playground

After lunch, Room 11, barred from sports and play-ing, huddled in little disgruntled groups on the playground for break.

"No running," muttered John to Smashie and Dontel. "What a waste of breaktime." He glared toward the opposite end of the playground, where Billy stood, pale and subdued, near a group of boys.

The nurse must not have thought he was very sick, thought Smashie.

It didn't look like the other kids were very happy to see him back.

"I think we better do something about all this," said John. He moved purposefully across the playground until he reached Alonso, who stood twirling his balaclava hat in his hands.

"Why do you think Billy won't confess?" Smashie asked Dontel.

Dontel shrugged. "Maybe he's telling the truth about not being the gluer."

"But there isn't anyone else in our class who would glue people to things! Let's go yell at him with John! Let's threaten to glue him to a ruler and see how he likes it! Let's make Scary Suits and leap out at him frighteningly for the rest of the week! Let's—"

"Smashie," said Dontel, "that isn't fair. There's no *proof* Billy did anything. You can't just punish someone because you think they might be guilty."

"Yes, I can," Smashie muttered, but she subsided. "You are right, Dontel. I got carried away. You know how that happens sometimes."

"Yes," said Dontel. "I do. Don't worry, Smashie. You keep things interesting."

"I try," Smashie admitted. "But I don't want to be mean."

"You're never mean, Smash," said Dontel. "Not like some people."

Smashie followed his gaze across the playground to where Mr Carper's hair tossed and quivered in the staffroom window.

"We are never free of Mr Carper," Smashie sighed. "It is just as bad as when we were in the canteen."

The staffroom had a window that looked into the canteen as well, and Mr Carper had sat directly in front of it as they ate, holding his milk carton up at various angles and peering around every few minutes to make faces in the window. It had taken Smashie some time to realize that he wasn't looking at them but rather practicing expressions in the window's reflection.

"He is probably in there telling the other teachers how awful we are," said Smashie grimly.

"More likely boasting about his chances of getting in the TrueYum circular," said Dontel.

Beyond the playground, the playing fields rang with the shouts of other, unpunished children.

John and some of the other members of Room 11 huddled to one side of their allotted area, plotting. Only Billy stood alone. Smashie felt a pang of sympathy for him. Still, she felt, if you are going to glue people to things, you have got to accept that people might get mad at you for it.

Kind of like when you say rude things about hamsters.

Smashie shook the thought away and shivered. "I'm kind of cold," she said.

"Probably because you forgot to bring your hoodie outside," said Dontel. He didn't add "again," for which Smashie was grateful.

"How can I warm up without it if we aren't allowed to run around?" she said. "I'm going to go get it!" And she dashed across the playground toward the building.

"My hoodie!" she called to the teacher on playground duty as she whizzed by. The teacher rolled her eyes but didn't blow her whistle.

Smashie burst through the door into the building.

"Watch where you're going!"

It was Cyrus and Willette, who were heading out to the playground. The two of them read to the year two classes every Tuesday at breaktime, and although Room 11 was on punishment, they had been permitted to read to them today.

"Sorry!" Smashie cried, and tore down the hall and into the empty classroom. Her steps slowed as soon as she was through the door.

Something about Room 11 was not right.

The back of Smashie's neck prickled.

The classroom certainly looked the same – tables, coat hooks, Ms Early's desk. But the very air of the room was changed. It was eerie, somehow. Spooky.

Smashie shivered. *Don't be silly,* she told herself firmly. *It is the same old Room 11. It's just weird because there are no kids in it.*

Right?

Smashie took a deep breath and gathered her courage. Then she dashed across the room as fast as she could, found her hoodie, and raced out the door, down the hall, and back out to the playground, heart pounding and chest heaving as she tried to catch her breath.

She entered a scene of no little confusion. Children were shouting and the teacher was shouting, too,

and blowing her whistle at the same time. The loudest shouts were coming from John and the group of boys in a corner of the playground.

"Help! Help!" cried a voice in the middle of their huddle.

It was Alonso Day.

"I've been glued to my balaclava hat!" he cried.

CHAPTER 7

A Terrible Discovery

All the children were furious once more and made no bones about the object of their anger.

"Why'd you have to go and do it again, Billy?" cried Jacinda as Mr Carper led the children back to Room 11. "We're already being punished!"

"Yeah!" cried John. "You'd better confess this time, Billy, or else."

"Yeah!"

"Yeah!"

The children waved their outerwear like pitchforks.

Billy slumped miserably before them.

"They've turned into an angry mob," said Dontel, his brows furrowed.

"Well, nobody likes to be glued to things," Smashie pointed out.

As if in response, Alonso brandished his hand with the balaclava hat stuck to it. "I don't want to live with my balaclava hat stuck to me for the rest of my life!" he cried.

"I didn't do it, Alonso," said Billy, his face pale, with circles under his eyes. "Honest."

The children grumbled.

"Hmmm," said Dontel.

"All right!" Mr Carper was all irritation. "Get in that room and get straight to work on your worksheets, all of you. Mrs Armstrong is already on her way down here to yell at you."

But the children were too angry to keep entirely quiet as they headed to the back of the room to their work boxes.

"Darned pest—"

"John has the right idea—"

"We'll make it so he *has* to confess—"

Mr Carper thumped Ms Early's desk. "What is the *matter* with you kids?"

"Nothing is wrong with us!"

"Yes, there is! I have a hat glued to me!"

"Come away from the back of the room imme-diately!" shouted the substitute. "I told you to stay *away* from that hamster! Take your seats at once and get to work!"

"But we can't help going near Patches, Mr Carper," said Willette. "We have to hang our coats up on our hooks."

"Well, do it faster, Girl with the Socks! Come on!"

"I should be feeding Patches right now," grumbled Siggie as he dug gingerly through his work box for his pencil. Since the episode with the tarantula, Siggie was always wary of what he might encounter in there. "He's supposed to get fresh water now, too!"

"Don't worry," Dontel reassured him as the rest of the children clattered away to their seats. "He'll be okay. We can ask Mr Bloom to give him some water after school."

Mr Bloom was the caretaker at the Rebecca Lee

Crumpler Primary School. His office was in a little building set apart from the main school, and it was a wonderful place, full of tools and back issues of *Extraterrestrial Times* and *Sky and Telescope* magazines.

"Suits me fine out here by myself," Mr Bloom always said. "I'd just as soon be off where no one can hear me! Play me a little music, have me a little lunch, think about alien life-forms. You kids know where to find me if I'm needed."

They certainly did. All the children looked forward to being asked to run and fetch Mr Bloom.

But the prospect did not cheer Siggie now. "It's not right to make Patches wait," he said, shaking loose some woolly fuzz clinging to his palm. "I bet he's awful thirsty."

He slid his gaze toward Patches's cage.

He froze, eyes wide with shock.

"Patches!" shouted Siggie.

"What's wrong?" cried Smashie.

Siggie swung toward her, wild-eyed. "It's Patches! He's gone!"

CHAPTER 8

Missing!

Siggie was right. Patches's cage stood just where it had always been. But Patches was not inside it.

The room erupted.

"Patches!" wailed Joyce. The other children took up the cry.

"Where could he be!"

"Did he escape?"

"If he escaped, we can catch him!"

"Shut the doors!"

"Patches!"

"Patches!"

"Everybody stop yelling!" Smashie shouted into the din. "If he's hiding, Patches will be too scared of all the noise to come out again!"

Dontel glanced at her, surprised.

"Just because I think he is blucky," said Smashie, "doesn't mean I want him to be scared. Or clobbered by somebody's feet."

"That is very nice, Smashie," said Dontel.

But Cyrus, for one, was not convinced of Smashie's niceness. "Since when do you care so much about Patches?" he asked.

"Yeah!" cried Joyce. "I bet you are secretly happy that Patches is gone!"

"I am not!" Smashie cried. Her cheeks burned. "That is unfair! I—"

But before she could defend herself further, Mr Carper bellowed from the front of the room, "ENOUGH!" He was purple with rage. "I have had it! Get away from there and sit down at once! All of you!"

"But, Mr Carper!" cried Jacinda.

"AT ONCE! Get to work on those worksheets.

In silence! The first person who talks or moves without permission is going to get it."

Roiling, the children sat.

Nobody could concentrate. Smashie's ears were still burning from Cyrus's and Joyce's words. And it wasn't just the two of them – other kids clearly agreed with their sentiments. Smashie had seen them glaring at her and nodding.

This is terrible! she thought. *The whole class is mad and thinking awful things about me! And I never even said a single rude thing to Patches!* Though she had, she admitted, said plenty of rude things *about* him.

Cheeks aflame, she picked up her work and read:

12. Another word for *sick* is _____.

CHAPTER 9

Uproar in Room 11

"ILL!"

The door to Room 11 had slammed open again, and Mrs Armstrong stood once more before the class, red faced and furious, her accidently apropos exclamation thundering over their heads.

Smashie put down her pencil.

"I am *more ill than ever*, Room 11! I am ILL IN MY BED WITH AN ICE BAG ON MY HEAD! *Twice* in one day I am called in to speak to you?"

"They're awful little things, aren't they?" said Mr Carper.

Mrs Armstrong cut him with an icy look.

"What exactly," she said, turning back to the children, "has gone on here?"

All of Room 11 began talking at once.

"Patches!"

"He's only tiny! Anybody could step on him!"

"He'll be hungry—"

"Frightened—"

"I'll have to go to university with a balaclava hat stuck to my hand!"

It was impossible to get a clear account of events.

Mrs Armstrong clapped her hands. "Stop this shouting at once!"

The children settled down. Eventually, from their broken sentences and the spectacle of Alonso, Mrs Armstrong understood that Room 11's class pet had gone missing and that, additionally, one of their number had been glued firmly to his balaclava hat.

"I am sorely disappointed in you, Room 11," she said. "*Sorely* disappointed! Particularly in you, Anonymous Glue Miscreant! How could you?

When the class is already on punishment?"

"One ... two ... three..." muttered John.

On "three," John and several other children turned and stared hard at Billy.

"What are you staring at me for?" he cried.

The starers gave no answer. Nor did they shift their gaze.

"We will deal with the matter of the glue momentarily," said Mrs Armstrong. "In the meantime, I know you are worried about your hamster." She gestured toward Patches's cage, empty and forlorn, behind them.

"Not all of us are worried," said Cyrus, glaring at Smashie.

"I am, too, worried!" The back of her neck grew hot as she confronted her classmates' angry eyes. "Why would you say I am not worried?"

"Because you kept saying how you didn't want Patches!" said Charlene.

"That doesn't mean I am glad he is gone!" cried Smashie despairingly.

"That's true, you guys," said Dontel. "You know she's not like that."

"Grr," snarled Joyce.

"I'm *not*!"

"At any rate," Mrs Armstrong continued, "I will ask Mr Bloom to look around very carefully as he goes through the building this afternoon." The head-mistress was sympathetic but firm. Smashie could scarcely pay attention. Her classmates were angrier at her than ever!

But even as she writhed under the weight of their unjust censure, a memory, as insistent as a hungry cat, was pricking at the back of Smashie's mind.

What was it? Something she had noticed when Siggie had discovered that Patches was missing. Something about Patches's cage.

Smashie had to look. Silently, she rose from her seat and made her way toward the back of the room.

"It is very sad, children, but this is part of what it means to own a pet," Mrs Armstrong said. "Perhaps you were not careful in latching the cage. Hamsters are sly little things—"

If by "sly" she means "yucky," Smashie couldn't help but think.

"And slipping away is something they do from time to time."

Smashie reached the cage that had, until very recently, housed her nemesis. In many ways, it looked just as it had this morning. Its metal bars were shiny and wood shavings lined the bottom. Patches's water bottle was still hooked to the side and his running wheel stood in the middle. But something was not right. It wasn't just that there was no *scrabble, scrabble, scrabble* of Patches's claws, or the fact that Patches did not seem like the sort of hamster who would strike out for adventure on his own. Something about the cage itself did not support the idea of a hamster who had just made good his escape. What was it?

In a flash, she knew.

"That's it!" Smashie cried, turning to face her classmates. "Excuse me, everybody!"

"Smashie McPepper! Who gave you permission to go back there?" Mr Carper was enraged. "Come away from that cage at once!"

"I'm sorry," said Smashie again. "But this is an emergency!"

"Smashie, what are you talking about?" asked Mrs Armstrong.

"The situation with Patches is much worse than we thought! Room 11, Patches did not escape!"

"What?"

"What do you mean?"

"I mean," said Smashie, "that Patches was stolen. And I can prove it!"

CHAPTER 10

Stolen!

Stolen!

"Smashie McPepper!" Mrs Armstrong clapped to signal silence.

I should really have on some kind of Discoverer's Suit, thought Smashie. But there was no time.

"His cage is latched *properly*, Mrs Armstrong. The hook is right through the loop on the outside. That means that someone – someone human – must have lifted the latch, taken him out, and then latched the cage up tight again! Patches couldn't have done that himself. Unless he is very, very smart—" Smashie swallowed to suppress her own views on the likelihood of Patches having a strong intellect—"or grew thumbs while we were at lunch. And we know he couldn't have grown thumbs!" Smashie gazed, wild-eyed, at her classmates. "That means someone took Patches out of his cage *on purpose!*"

"But why?" cried Charlene.

"And how?" cried Siggie.

"Hey!" Alonso cried plaintively over the din. "Couldn't someone unglue me while we talk about all this?"

"I can." Dontel went to the sink, where he moistened some paper towels and headed toward Alonso. Smashie joined him at the intersection of boy and balaclava hat, and they started trying to loosen the glue's grasp.

"Nice thinking, Smashie," Dontel said as the other children buzzed with excited conversation all around them.

"Thank you, Dontel," said Smashie.

"ROOM 11!" Mrs Armstrong was beside herself. "Things have gone beyond the pale. What has gotten into all of you? Imagine behaving like this while your teacher is out! People gluing people! Hamsters getting stolen! Ms Early will be as ill about it all as I am – ILL IN BED WITH AN IV DRIP at the way Room 11 has conducted itself in her absence!"

"Alonso," said Dontel beneath Mrs Armstrong's shouting, "you are pretty stuck. Water isn't going to do the trick. I am going to have to use my mayonnaise." He reached into his pocket.

"Mayonnaise?" Alonso asked, startled.

"Mayonnaise has vinegar in it. And vinegar is a solvent," Dontel explained. "It will loosen the glue's hold on you."

"Dontel is always right about things like that," Smashie assured Alonso. "You can trust him."

"I know." Alonso nodded. "Do what you have to, Dontel."

Dontel squeezed the packet, and he and Smashie began to scrub once more.

"I feel like a salad," said Alonso.

At the front of the room, Mrs Armstrong wrung her hands.

"I knew that hamster would be nothing but trouble," said Mr Carper.

Mrs Armstrong glanced at him, then drew herself up. "We will stop this discussion for now, Room 11," she said. "But tomorrow, I shall confer with Ms Early and together we will devise your further punishment."

"What's happened to our room?" cried Joyce. "First we had a gluer and now we have a hamster swiper! I never want to come back here again!"

"Me, either!"

The feeling was palpable. Room 11 was a troubled room indeed.

"Don't worry, Room 11!" cried Smashie. "I am sure Patches will be okay!"

There were snorts from all corners of Room 11.

"Sure," said Joyce. "Because you're real cut up about him, Smash."

"Stop," said Smashie, "I *am*! Didn't I just figure out about him being stolen?"

"What do you care if he was?" cried Willette. "You're just glad you don't have to see his feet anymore!"

A lump rose in Smashie's throat. She met Dontel's concerned eyes over Alonso's balaclava'd hand.

What if people stayed mad at her for the whole rest of the year? Lunches alone and no playdates except with Dontel, nobody else believing that Smashie was kind – Smashie's very acceptance as a member of Room 11 was on the line.

She blinked hard and swallowed. What could she do?

Plenty, that's what.

Smashie squared her shoulders. Dontel nodded at her and thrust out his own chest. Their minds were as one.

"We are going to have to investigate," said Smashie.

"Yes," Dontel agreed. "And bring the thief to justice."

CHAPTER 11

Planning an Investigation Suit

Mrs Armstrong left and Alonso was at last free from his hat, although he smelled something like a sandwich. Smashie's mind was working like sixty, planning the upcoming investigation.

"We'll have to muster every bit of our thinking power," she whispered to Dontel. "We will have to have special Investigation Suits! With a lot of places for storing clues and pencils."

"I think I'll just wear my regular clothes," Dontel

whispered back. "I can put clues and my pencil in my pockets."

"Clues are different from the stuff you normally collect in your pockets, Dontel."

"Not really," said Dontel. "Clues are things you analyze to see what you can learn from them, right? That is exactly what I do with my pocket stuff!"

"That's true," said Smashie, considering. "Then you've spent your whole life gathering clues, Dontel! You are already an investigator!"

Mr Carper sat at Ms Early's desk and stared at the ceiling.

"I'm not kidding, kids," he said to the light fixture. "One word from one person in this class and I will pop. Just get to work, all of you. Eventually, this godforsaken day must end."

"I think we'll have to do our investigating kind of quietly," said Dontel. "Discreetly. Otherwise, who-ever stole Patches will be on their guard around us and we won't be able to get at the truth."

"That's a good point." Sadly, Smashie gave up her imaginings about dazzling her classmates with a sweeping entrance into Room 11 tomorrow in her

Investigation Suit. "I guess I will have to tell people that my Investigation Suit is just a regular Thinking Suit."

"Yes," said Dontel. "I think you will."

At the next table, John gave a low, careful cough. "One, two, three," he muttered.

Immediately, John and his cohorts turned and stared again at Billy, who bowed his head and looked miserably at his paper.

"Poor guy," said Dontel.

"Tchah," said Smashie.

At the table beside Smashie and Dontel's, Jacinda was sniffling. "Who would take such a precious little angel?" she gulped.

John and Cyrus shook their heads.

"Someone down-deep mean," said Cyrus.

"You said it," said John.

"You think it was Billy?" asked Cyrus.

John looked thoughtful. "Nah," he said at last. "Billy's a trick player, not a thief."

Cyrus looked at Billy's ashen, miserable face. "That's true. Plus," he said, "the kid looks like he's about to throw up."

"You should stop staring at him, then," said Smashie.

John rolled his eyes at her.

"Cut the chat," Mr Carper said, his head snapping down to glare at them. He got up.

Sighing, Smashie began to sketch ideas for her Investigation Suit in the margins of her completed packet.

Grammy's wide hat, she planned. *That green one with the plaid band. I can modify the brim to hold clues. And I'll need some kind of sash.*

NO.1 DETECTIVE

She could talk it over with her mother. Smashie's mother had a pretty good eye when it came to suits.

"What's this?"

Whoosh! Smashie's paper was snatched from the table and flew up over her head.

Mr Carper was beside her. "Drawing all over your worksheet?"

"I finished is why, Mr Carper," said Smashie. "I was drawing quietly."

"You finished? For real?" Mr Carper glanced down the page. "It's messy, Ears. Go back and make it look good." He slapped her paper back down. "Being quick is overrated, kids," he said. "Believe me, sometimes you can be too smart for your own good."

The class gasped.

"That's not what Ms Early says, Mr Carper," said Dontel. "She says that in order to be good people and good citizens, we have to be as smart as we can. She says it is wrong not to use and develop the brains you were born with, and she's never more proud of us than when we're smart."

"Or kind," Jacinda added.

"Or kind," Dontel agreed. "She says—"

"Blah and blah, of course, how true," said Mr Carper. "Let's just get through the rest of the day, okay, Boy with the Elbows?"

All of the boys in the class looked puzzledly at their arms.

"He means me," said Dontel.

Smashie drew in an outraged breath. "Mr Carper," she began.

This time it was John who shook his head. "Pick your battles, Smashie," he said. "The day's almost done."

Dontel was pretending to still be working on his own completed worksheet as Mr Carper continued his stroll around the class. "Want to meet at my house after school?" Dontel asked Smashie. My grandma won't mind, and we have a lot to talk about."

"Check," said Smashie.

Dontel looked at her.

"That was me using Investigator Language."

"Oh," said Dontel. They grinned at each other.

Mr Carper passed by Patches's cage. "Horrifying," he muttered.

"Does he mean us or hamsters?" whispered Willette.

"Sweet heaven," said Mr Carper, reaching the front of the room and taking a look at his reflection in the top of a tin of mints, "this day has aged me." He passed his hand faintly through his hair.

CHAPTER 12

A Dire Prediction

"This was a terrible day of school," Smashie said to Dontel as they packed up their things to go home. "All this glue plus everybody upset about Patches!"

"*Almost* everybody," Dontel said, waggling his brows knowingly at Smashie.

"Hey!" she cried, wounded.

"Sorry, Smash." Dontel was contrite. "I was just playing."

Mrs Armstrong appeared firmly in the doorway.

"Everybody out and to the buses this minute. I'm locking Room 11!"

"Locking Room 11?" Mr Carper asked, his eyebrows skating to the top of his head.

"Indeed. I am not having any more pranks. I am sorry to hurry you as well, Mr Carper, but I have a meeting directly after school and would like this taken care of forthwith."

"But..." Mr Carper gestured at Ms Early's desk. "I've got a lot of things to get together. The kids' packets and whatnot."

"I already made them into a pile for you, Mr Carper," said Charlene.

Mr Carper ignored her. "And I'd hate to leave the place untidy," he said.

"We've done our end-of-the-day jobs, Mr Carper," said Alonso.

"I'd be glad to lock up for you when I leave, Mrs Armstrong," said Mr Carper. "You could just leave me the key."

"No, actually, I could not," said Mrs Armstrong briskly. "I'm afraid it's everybody out. All right, Room 11! Form a line!"

Dripping papers and his jacket and several combs, an irritated Mr Carper led the students out to the pavement, where walkers and children who were picked up from school turned right, and Smashie and Dontel and the rest of the bus children turned left.

"I'm cold," said Smashie in the bus line.

Dontel sighed. "Hoodie."

"Ugh!" Smashie smacked her forehead. "Again! I was too busy planning about my suit!"

"Go on," said Dontel. "I'll make sure the bus doesn't leave without you."

Smashie raced back to the room and ran into Mrs Armstrong, who was standing at the door with Smashie's hoodie in her hand.

Smashie gulped. "Thanks, Mrs Armstrong."

"Hrmm," said the headmistress, one eyebrow raised.

Smashie took her hoodie.

Mr Potter, the bus driver, was looking irritated as Smashie boarded the waiting bus at last, thrusting her arms into the soft sleeves of her hoodie.

"I'm sorry, Mr Potter!" cried Smashie. "I am really going to work on not forgetting things."

"So your friend said," said Mr Potter.

"Thank you very much for waiting for me."

"Sit down, Smashie."

Smashie sat down.

Mr Potter threw the bus into gear. "Someday," he said, pulling out, "this is all going to catch up with you, Smashie McPepper."

"That's what my grammy says, too, Mr Potter."

"Hmmm," said Mr Potter, and drove on.

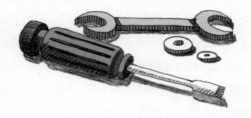

CHAPTER 13

Investigating

"Grammy!"

"I'm in here! By the washer!"

Still breathing hard from her dash home from the bus stop, Smashie raced toward her grandmother's voice.

Grammy was crouched beside the washing machine, a screwdriver in one hand and a library book called *Fixing Your Fix-Its!* open in the other.

Smashie stopped short. "I thought you fixed the washer yesterday, Grammy," she said.

"I did." Grammy sighed. "Now I have to fix what I fixed."

"Don't worry, Grammy," said Smashie. "I always wind up having to fix things I fixed."

"It is this family's fatal flaw," her grandmother agreed, and sat up. "Hello, Smashie."

"Hello, Grammy."

"How was your day?"

Smashie threw up her arms. "Awful! So awful I have to go to Dontel's right now! May I, please?"

Her grandmother looked at Smashie over the top of her glasses. "I don't like the sound of that," she said.

Smashie jigged up and down. "I wasn't *bad*, Grammy. It's only that a lot of terrible things happened at once. Dontel and I have to figure things out! Please, can I go?"

Her grandmother pulled herself up to her feet. "I suppose." She exhaled, closing her book over her thumb to hold her place. "If you behave yourself. You're a handful, Smashie McPepper, and I don't want you going over there and tiring Lorraine Marquise out."

Lorraine Marquise was Dontel's grandmother.

"I am not a handful!" Smashie cried. "Mostly all what I do is thinking!"

"It's when the thinking is over," her grandmother said darkly, "and you get to the *doing* part that things get a little shaky."

Smashie had to admit that this was, perhaps, a little bit true.

Nonetheless, permission was permission. "Thank you, Grammy!" she said and raced to the door.

She raced back.

"Did *you* have a nice day?" she asked.

"I did," said her grandmother, already back on the floor by the washer. "Lorraine and I put in a full morning reading to people at the library and then we had the girls over for whist. And now I'm tackling this washer. I call that a good, productive day."

"Me too," said Smashie. "I'm glad you had a good day, Grammy."

And she bounded across the street to Dontel's.

"I've got crackers and cheese all ready for us," said Dontel as he opened the door for Smashie.

"That is very good," said Smashie. "We need to fortify ourselves for our investigation." And they tucked into their salty snack with gusto.

"You kids clean up your crumbs when you're done," said Dontel's grandmother, who was sitting by the window with a mystery story. She had been a nurse practitioner for many years and now that she was retired, she was reading her way through the library's mystery section, author by author. "Mice might appreciate them, but I surely don't."

"We will, Grandma," Dontel promised.

"We will, Mrs Marquise," said Smashie. "Thank you for having me."

"My pleasure, Smashie. Speaking of mice," said Mrs Marquise, "didn't you all just get a little mouse for your class pet? How's the little mister doing? He must be as cute as a button."

"Patches is a hamster, Grandma, not a mouse," said Dontel. "And he *was* cute."

"Was?"

Dontel swallowed a bite of cracker. "He's missing. Today. Gone right out of his cage. We don't know where he is."

Grandma tutted. "That's a shame," she said.

"Yes," said Dontel. "But me and Smashie are going to find him."

"Good," said Mrs Marquise. "Why don't you take some of that cheese to school and lay it out for him in his cage? He'll sneak right back in to get it."

"We are a little worried he might not be in our room anymore, though, Grandma."

"It's a real mystery, Mrs Marquise," said Smashie. "Dontel and I have to investigate."

"That's the right thing to do," said Mrs Marquise. "Seeing's how you all are so fond of him."

Dontel said nothing, but his eyes grinned at Smashie over his cracker.

Smashie was aggrieved. "I am about to work very hard for Patches's safe return, Dontel!"

Mrs Marquise frowned at her book. "I hope you two use your brains more than the detective in this story," she said. "He drives me wild! In every one of the books he's in, he runs all over the place looking for clues but he never makes any kind of plan. And the only way he ever solves a mystery is by chance – he just happens to overhear the culprit boasting about his crime, or he stumbles on him and catches him in the act." She shook her head. "I prefer a real, thinking detective. Not one that just relies on luck."

"I agree with you, Mrs Marquise," said Smashie.

"Me too," said Dontel. "Why do you read those, Grandma? If the detective is so bad?"

"I have a little crush on his sidekick," Grandma admitted. "He's a wonderful young man."

"Ugh," said Dontel. "Well, don't worry, Grandma. We're going to use our heads."

"Good," said Mrs Marquise. "That's what I like to hear." Then she was lost in her novel again, tutting away at the latest example of the detective's shoddy methods.

"All right!"

Crackers eaten, Smashie and Dontel settled in the living room. Smashie loved the Marquises' living room, which smelled sweetly of the fresh flowers Dontel's father arranged in vases each week. She was excited to begin. "Let's start having ideas!"

"Yes," said Dontel. "Only let's be methodical about it."

Despite the recent conversation with Mrs Marquise, Smashie waved methodicalness away with an airy hand. "Let's just use our imaginations! I have got lots of thoughts. First we can find out if anybody was wearing a sneaky, all-black Thief Suit today. Then we can investigate to see if anybody keeps a mask in their work box to disguise themselves! Or if there was a trail of hamster food on the floor, luring Patches to freedom. Or—"

"That is a lot of ideas to keep track of, Smashie. I think my grandma is right. We have to be smart about this." Dontel reached into one of the desk drawers and took out two small spiral notebooks. "We need notebooks. Investigation Notebooks."

"Oooh," said Smashie pleasurably. "Notebooks!"

Both notebooks were squat and colorful. One had FIRST STREET BAPTIST written across the front, and the other featured an earnest-looking horse.

"Could I please use the horse one?" asked Smashie.

"Sure." Dontel handed it over.

Smashie looked at the cover and sighed. "A horse would have been a terrific class pet."

"Yes," said Dontel. "Except that I'm allergic to them."

"I was forgetting," said Smashie. "Then it would be a terrible pet. You would have to blow your nose all day long."

"Yep," said Dontel, taking up the other notebook. "Let's get to business. Let's start by writing down the facts as we know them."

"Good idea," said Smashie, and flipped to the first page of her notebook and began to write.

THE FACTS AS WE KNOW THEM
1. Patches was in his cage all morning until lunch.
We know this because we saw him when we
got to school.

"Also because he makes that *scrabble, scrabble, scrabble* sound," said Smashie, showing the page to Dontel. "We could hear that from our seats even after morning break."

"Plus I could see him from our table," said Dontel.

"I am willing to testify that I saw Patches in his cage until lunch."

"Swell," said Smashie. "Let's put that down."

WITNESS TO FACT #1: Dontel Marquise

They continued:

2. Patches was missing when we got back to our room after lunch.

WITNESSES TO FACT #2: the whole class

CONCLUSION: Patches was stolen when our class was out of the room for lunch.

"Those are some solid facts," said Dontel, pleased. "And a nice piece of logic, too."

"Yes," Smashie agreed. "And we have the time of the theft narrowed down to between twelve o'clock, when we left Room 11 for lunch, and twelve forty, when we came back."

"Let's write that down, too."

They added the fact to their notes.

"Now," said Dontel, "we have to put our mind to the *who*."

"Yes," said Smashie. "We have to think about what kind of person would be a hamster swiper."

"I was thinking," said Dontel, "that there are two kinds of people who might take Patches. One is a person who would do it as a prank. And the other is a person who would do it to be mean."

"It could also have been a person who is a crazed scientist who has always wanted to be a hamster and stole Patches to swap brains with him," said Smashie.

Dontel gave her a level look.

"Oh, fine," said Smashie. "We can do the reasons you said first."

"Are you sure?"

"Certainly."

"Thank you."

"That is okay."

"If it were a mean person," said Dontel, "who do you think it could be?"

"Nobody," said Smashie. "Except for when they are mad at you, we have a very nice class."

"That is true," said Dontel. "Well, what about if it were a prank?"

"There is always Billy," said Smashie. "And some of his pranks *are* kind of mean."

Dontel agreed. "I guess he is a good suspect."

"A suspect! I love Investigator Language!" Smashie flipped open to a new page. "Let's make a list of all the inspector words we get to use in the course of our investigation."

"Swell idea, Smash! We could write them in the back of our notebooks."

"For easy reference!" Smashie nodded. She turned to the last page of her notebook and busied herself with her pencil.

INVESTIGATOR LANGUAGE
1. Suspect

"Let's put *detective* and *investigate* down, too," said Dontel. "We've been using those a lot."

"Good idea," said Smashie, and added them to her list:

2. Detective
3. Investigate

"Now," said Smashie, "we can get back to the investigation. Let's start another list. For suspects."

SUSPECT LIST
1. Billy Kamarski

But as soon as she was done writing the name, Smashie leaned back and shook her head. "I don't really think it is him this time, though. If Billy did it, he would be happier. Whenever he does a prank, he does that thing where he covers his mouth with his hand and gets all chumped up with laughing behind it until we realize it is him."

"That's true," said Dontel. "And all day today, he only looked awful."

"Well, because everybody was mad at him for the glue," said Smashie.

"Maybe," said Dontel. "But maybe your thing about why he wouldn't have done the hamster makes him not be the glue person, either. He didn't boast about that, right?"

"Dontel," said Smashie reasonably, "nobody else does tricks like that all the time. No one else would think gluing people was such a good joke, either. Think of all of Billy's phone calls. The tarantula. That time John was a pirate for Halloween and he marched through the whole Halloween parade with that sign Billy pinned to his back that said, YO-HO-HO AND A BOTTLE OF DUMB."

"Hmm," said Dontel. "I don't know."

"Blah and blah," said Smashie.

"*Blah and blah?*" said Dontel. "You sound like Mr Carper."

"Ugh!" cried Smashie. "I will never say *blah and blah* again!" And she fell back to the floor and lifted her feet in the air in despair.

"Well, we should figure out how we will investigate Billy, anyhow," said Dontel. "Just to be sure."

"Wait! Ugh!" cried Smashie. "We can't investigate Billy!" She let her feet drop with a tremendous thump.

"What's going on in there?" Mrs Marquise called.

"Nothing!" Dontel called back.

"It was only me, thumping, Mrs Marquise!" Smashie shouted. "I will stop!"

"Thank you," replied Mrs Marquise.

Smashie sat up.

"I only thumped because I realized that we are dumb, Dontel," said Smashie. "Billy can't be the hamster swiper. He was sick at the nurse's office at lunchtime, remember?"

"Ugh," said Dontel. "You're right. He was all green around the gills. And then after the nurse, he was back outside with us."

"Rats," said Smashie. "There goes the suspect list."

Taking up their pencils, Smashie and Dontel crossed out Billy's name.

"Curses," said Smashie. "Investigating is hard."

"Ugh!"

"Ugh!"

Mrs Marquise appeared in the doorway. "What is all this 'ugh' yelling?" she asked.

"Sorry, Mrs Marquise," said Smashie. "I got carried away about our mystery. But don't worry – I'm working on not getting so carried away."

"I'm happy to hear that, Smashie," said Mrs Marquise. "But I'm sure my grandson was in the thick of things, too. My goodness, but I never knew two children to squawk and raise a ruckus like the two of you. Dontel, don't you forget you still have your homework to do. And your mother and father are planning on Family Game Night tonight."

"I won't forget, Grandma. Me and Smashie are going to work on our mystery for just another couple of minutes. Then we'll do our homework."

"Good," said Mrs Marquise. "I'll be in the kitchen if you need help."

"Thank you, Grandma."

"Thanks, Mrs Marquise."

"Oh, well," said Smashie when Mrs Marquise had gone. "I guess we will have to come up with a list of mad scientists after all."

CHAPTER 14
A New Suspect

The rest of the afternoon was not successful in terms of useful investigating, but the next morning, Smashie was ready to go. She and Dontel had plans to meet up at Smashie's house before the bus came. At last he arrived, and Smashie flung open the door to greet him.

"That is some suit," said Dontel, taking her in.

"Yes." Smashie beamed. If she had ever needed a suit to help her think, it was now. She had torn through the house like a wild thing the evening before, looking for things to turn into her Investigation Suit. Thus, this morning she stood somewhat lost in the fabric of a blue hot-suit from Grammy's go-go dancing days, the legs and sleeves rolled up and the surplus around her middle bound with a belt she had made out of an old macramé sash. From the belt dangled pouches in which she planned to keep clues and supplies. Grammy had refused to let Smashie modify her wide-brimmed hat, so Smashie had taken a flat golfing visor from her mother's cupboard instead and built extra places along the sides into which she could tuck more clues.

Her mother had not minded about the visor, but she had been terribly upset that she hadn't been included in the making of Smashie's latest creation.

"Is that a suit?" she had cried this morning when Smashie came down.

"Of course it's a suit," said her grandmother, eyeing Smashie over her coffee.

"Smashie!" said her mother. "You know how much I enjoy helping to make your suits!"

It was true. A firm believer in the power of a hot-glue gun and a roll of tape, Mrs McPepper liked

to make things as much as Smashie did and she supported Smashie's suit making completely. "There is nothing like a suit to turn a frown upside down, Smashie," she often said.

"I truly am sorry, Mum," said Smashie. "But sometimes I have got to make them on my own."

"Well," said her mother, disappointed, "I don't know about those pouches. At any rate, don't forget your lunch. I've put two cupcakes in yours, but one is for Dontel. Be sure you give it to him, please."

"I will."

Now, with Mrs McPepper gone to work and her grandmother safely back with the washing machine, Smashie led Dontel to the kitchen table and handed him an identical sash full of pouches she had made for him to wear.

"It's not a full suit," said Smashie. "But I thought this would be useful. It would show we are partners."

"Um, thank you," said Dontel. "But I think I'll just stick with looking regular. People might ask questions if I turn up with a bunch of pouches all over me. I don't want to blow our cover, remember?"

"Oh," said Smashie, looking at her enpouched stomach. "Do you think this looks too much like an Investigator Suit?"

"Nah," said Dontel. "You wear all kinds of different suits, all the time. No one will think anything of it."

"Good," said Smashie, cheering. But then her brow furrowed. She took out her notebook, across the top of which she had printed:

INVESTIGATION NOTEBOOK
THE CASE OF WHAT HAPPENED TO PATCHES THE HAMSTER

"I guess I should cross that out."

"I think that would be good," Dontel agreed. "Here, I've got a Sharpie in my pocket."

Smashie crossed out the words.

"Smashie," said Dontel, "I woke up with an idea."

"You did?"

"Yes."

"About a new suspect?"

"Yes."

"Who?"

Dontel looked at her gravely.

"Mr Carper."

"Mr *Carper*?" Smashie cried, scarcely able to believe her ears.

"Yes," said Dontel. "I think we need to investigate him."

"Hooray!" cried Smashie. "We can perform a citizen's arrest!" An immensely attractive picture of her in her Investigation Suit and Dontel in his normal clothes frog-marching the hapless Mr Carper downtown to the authorities filled Smashie's mind. "Oh, I am so happy," she said. "He'll regret that he was ever mean about people being smart!"

"That is true," said Dontel.

"Investigating is the best!" said Smashie. "I never thought we would get to foil Mr Carper as well! You have the most terrific ideas, Dontel. We always knew Mr Carper was a big villain!"

"Yes," said Dontel. "But I was also thinking about it in terms of the kind of person who would be likely to steal Patches."

Smashie's mouth fell open. "Do you think Mr Carper is a mad scientist in disguise?"

"No," said Dontel. "I don't. But I think there are other reasons someone could have done it. First of all, Mr Carper doesn't like hamsters."

"Yes," said Smashie. "He snarled at Patches the whole time. He called him a disease carrier."

"Right," said Dontel. "In other words, he would be glad to be rid of him. That's what they call a *motive*."

"Ooh," said Smashie. "I am adding that to our list of Investigator Language! And then," she said darkly, "I am adding Mr Carper to our list of suspects."

"Me too," said Dontel. And he took out his list.

INVESTIGATOR LANGUAGE
1. Suspect
2. Detective
3. Investigate
4. Motive

Next they turned to their suspect lists and updated those as well:

SUSPECT LIST

1. ~~Billy Kamarski~~
2. Mr Carper
MOTIVE: Hating Patches

"Dontel." Smashie's eyes were wide. "We've been thinking that whoever took Patches out of that cage put him somewhere else. But Mr Carper would probably just—"

Dontel laid his hand on her shoulder. "Let's take it slow," he said. He looked very serious. "We'll think it through. Our number-one goal is the safe return of Patches, but regardless—" Dontel swallowed.

"We have got to bring the thief to justice," said Smashie.

"Yes," said Dontel. "Now, let's make sure we are on the right track."

But Smashie was still caught up in the excitement of an impending kerfuffle. "Here's what we'll do," she plotted. "We'll call him up with our voices disguised and tell him we know where some treasure is buried. Then, when he goes to the place with his shovel, we will leap out and arrest him! It will be like putting cheese in the cage for Patches, only it will be pretend treasure instead of cheese, and Mr Carper instead of a hamster!"

Dontel stared at her, then collapsed backward into a chair. He smacked his forehead.

"UGH!" he cried. "UGH!" He clapped his hands over his eyes.

"What's going on in there?" Smashie's grandmother called.

"Nothing!" Smashie called back.

"Dumb!" cried Dontel.

Smashie turned back to Dontel's hand-covered face. "You think he won't believe us about the treasure?" she asked, crestfallen. "And quit calling me dumb."

"I would never call you dumb," said Dontel. "The treasure is a great idea. I meant *I'm* dumb. For even thinking about Mr Carper." He dropped his hands and looked at Smashie. "We already figured out that whoever did it had to have gone into our classroom during lunch."

"Yes," said Smashie. "Mr Carper could have done that with no problem. Nobody would question whether he belonged in Room 11 since he was our teacher for the day!"

"Yes," said Dontel. "But Smashie, we know he *didn't* go into the classroom during lunch. He was in the staffroom the whole time. We *saw* him. Remember?"

The memory of Mr Carper's ruff of curls in the staffroom windows, both inside and out, rose in Smashie's mind.

"Rats." Smashie was deflated. "Are you sure you saw him there even when I left to get my hoodie?"

"Yes," said Dontel. "I did."

"Pleh! Then you are right."

"Mr Carper," said Dontel sadly, "is in the clear."

Slowly, they crossed out Mr Carper's name.

SUSPECT LIST

1. ~~Billy Kamarski~~

2. ~~Mr Carper~~

Then they added:

WITNESSES TO IT NOT BEING POSSIBLE
IT WAS MR CARPER: Us.

"I am very disappointed," said Smashie.

"Me too," said Dontel.

"We have had two suspects," said Smashie. "And we have had to cross them both out."

"I think," said Dontel, "that maybe we are a little bit terrible at investigating."

"Maybe I need to make a better suit."

They stared morosely at the floor.

"That's a pretty intense suit already, Smashie McPepper," said her grandmother, coming unexpectedly into the kitchen. She looked a bit harassed, with a smudge of oil on her nose. "However, I will say that hot-suit had a different effect when I wore it as a girl. Hop along to the bus stop, now, you two. It's almost time."

CHAPTER 15

An Awful Realization

Mr Potter, the bus driver, raised his eyes at Smashie's outfit but said only, "Sit down, Smashie."

"Yes, Mr Potter."

As he did every morning, Dontel opened his lunch box and began to consume the sandwich meant for his lunch.

"Smashie," he said, swallowing a mouthful of ham, "you went back in the room to get your hoodie during lunch. Maybe you saw a clue without knowing it. Think! Did you see anything suspicious?"

Smashie furrowed her brow.

Nobody in a Thief Suit. No muffled sounds as if from a hiding doer of wrong. No evil cackles as if from a successful mad scientist.

"No," she said regretfully. "I didn't see anything at all. I didn't hear anything, either. The room was empty."

"Heck." Dontel slumped back to the floor. "This is going to be tough."

But as he spoke, the eerie feeling Smashie had had yesterday when she'd gone back to Room 11 crept up her spine again, and she shuddered. "I forgot to tell you, though," she said slowly. "Because we got all caught up in Alonso's hand and then Patches. But it *was* strange in Room 11, when I went back for my hoodie. Spooky, almost. Like something was wrong."

"Wrong?"

"Yes," said Smashie. "It was almost *too* quiet."

"Hmmm," said Dontel, furrowing his brow. "Was the feeling to do with Patches at all? Did you see him at that point? Was he still in his cage?"

"That is hard to say," said Smashie. "You know I kind of avoid him." She felt badly admitting it, but it was true. "I didn't even think to look. I was kind of spooked, so I was just focused on getting my hoodie."

"Rats."

Smashie nodded. Then she gasped.

"Wait!" she cried. "Dontel! Patches *must* have been gone by then!"

"What do you mean, Smashie?"

"It really *was* too quiet! No *scrabble, scrabble, scrabble* sounds!" Smashie was triumphant. "That must have been what made it feel so eerie! And Patches couldn't have been asleep, because I was very loud when I first came in. I was running on account of I didn't want the teacher to get mad at me. And you know how frighty Patches is. He'd never have been able to sleep through me running all the way through to the back of the room!"

"Maybe all the noise you were making masked his scrabbling noises."

Smashie shook her head. "No. Because I didn't make any noise when I looked through my work box. I only made soft hoodie-moving sounds. I'm sure I would have heard him!"

"That makes a lot of sense, Smashie!" Dontel's eyes were bright. He put away his sandwich and fished his Investigation Notebook out of his backpack. "So somebody must have snatched Patches between the start of lunch and about ten minutes into break."

"Yes," said Smashie, extracting her own Investigation Notebook from her sash. "That means between noon and twelve twenty-five. Oh, we are so good at investigating! Let's write that down!"

And they added the information enthusiastically to their notes.

"It is too bad we have to exonerate Mr Carper," said Dontel. "Because otherwise he fits perfectly."

"Exonerate," breathed Smashie pleasurably, and she added the word to her list.

"Mr Carper had access *and* motive. Who else could have both?"

"Dontel, you are excellent at Investigator Language," said Smashie. "Let's write down *access* on the word list, too."

"All right." They did.

"Now, let's think," said Smashie.

"Who had access to the room when no one else was there?" Dontel began.

Smashie joined in. "And who also hates hamsters—?"

She broke off.

"What?" said Dontel.

Smashie gulped. She blinked her eyes rapidly.

"Dontel!" she whispered.

It couldn't be.

But there was nothing to be done for it.

Sadly, underneath her heading *Suspect List*, Smashie carefully printed:

3. Me

CHAPTER 16

Unpleasant Self-Reflection

"We have to launch a full investigation," said Smashie miserably. "We have to question me closely."

"Smashie, it was not you!"

"How do we know?" Smashie wailed. "Maybe the kids are right and I am as awful as they think! Maybe I just don't remember! I forget things all the time! Look at how I am with my hoodie! This is exactly what Mr Potter was warning me about yesterday on the bus," she said, flinging an arm toward the front of the bus. "It is all catching up with me!"

"Smashie, you forget things like hoodies and permission slips," said Dontel. "You don't forget things you *do*."

"I do, too!" cried Smashie. "I forget things I do all the time! I was so busy thinking about ideas for a Bug-Luring Suit once that I put a yogurt away in my dresser instead of the fridge, and I only realized it a week later, when it got smelly! I forget other things, too, like to set the table when my mother asks me to and where I put the mail when I came in from school. I—"

Her mind was a tornado.

She must have crept through the darkened school, she thought. Maybe she had even had a Thief Suit on! While she was snatching her hoodie from its spot, her hand must have crept out toward Patches's cage and—

"The class is right to hate me!" she cried.

"They are not!" Dontel's voice was insistent. "Smashie! You can't be the wrongdoer!"

"Yes, I can be! We can't be put off the trail of me just because we like me!"

"Smashie." Dontel took her shoulders in his hands and looked into her eyes. "You could not possibly be the thief."

"Of course I could! I fit the clues exactly! Why wouldn't it be me?"

"Because," said Dontel in low, burning tones, "you are scared of Patches's feet."

Smashie stared at Dontel.

"You would never, ever touch him," Dontel continued. "Not on purpose. You would be too worried about touching his feet! Even if you wanted Patches gone more than anything, I don't believe your scaredness would let you pick him up and take him."

Smashie sat frozen, staring hard at her friend.

"You are right, Dontel," she said at last. "I *am* very frightened of Patches's feet. I would rather do most anything than touch them."

"That's what I'm saying!" said Dontel.

But Smashie was not ready to let herself off the hook just yet.

"But what about me being so forgetful?" she asked.

"You never, ever forget things you *think*, Smashie. And stealing Patches would have taken a lot of thinking. It is nothing like that yogurt situation."

"I do always remember about things I think," Smashie admitted. "I remember things you think, too, Dontel."

Dontel nodded.

"Yes," he said. "You do. Come on, Smash. Let's strike you off the list."

"All right," said Smashie. And with a tremendous sense of relief, she crossed herself out.

"I think," said Dontel, "we'd better calm down with our thinking."

He was right. Smashie dearly loved letting her thoughts run away with her, but sometimes, like now, they ran too far and when they did, it was awful. It was just very hard to tell in the moment, sometimes, which way it was going to go.

"Thank you for clearing my name, Dontel," she said.

"No problem," Dontel replied. "I got your back, you got mine."

CHAPTER 17

Back to Normal?

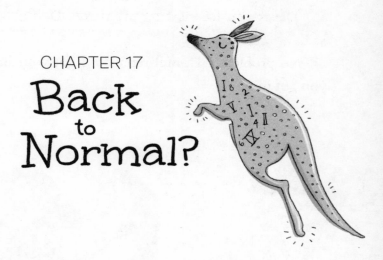

The bus ride over, Smashie and Dontel stood outside the doors to the Rebecca Lee Crumpler Primary School with the rest of Room 11, waiting for the bell to signal that it was time to enter the building.

Joyce was standing at the foot of the steps, her pink backpack on her back.

"Hello, Joyce," said Smashie.

Joyce raised her chin. "I'm going to go stand with Willette," she said, deliberately not looking at

Smashie. "*She* understands how I'm feeling about Patches."

And off she clomped.

Smashie's shoulders slumped.

"Just remember we're working on it," said Dontel comfortingly, his hand on her shoulder. "The kids'll come around."

"Not if we don't solve this case." Smashie's voice was troubled.

John Singletary came up beside Dontel. "Marquise," he greeted him.

"Singletary." Dontel nodded back.

"Don't look now," John said, "but Mr Awful is back."

He was right. Mr Carper was leaning against the building nearby, talking to Miss Dismont. "Big day today, huh?" he was saying. "What with the TrueYum nutrition assembly."

"I suppose," said Miss Dismont. Miss Dismont was a beautiful woman in her mid-fifties, plump with a loaf of curly red hair and a pair of kangaroo earrings dangling from her ears. Miss Dismont was famous for her love of kangaroos. The earrings were

just one of her many marsupial-themed accessories.
Kangaroos leaped across her curls on shining hair
clips and sprang across the tote bag in which she carried her books and papers. Even the license plate on
her convertible read, KANGA-RU. But best of all, during
the hour her class had mathematics each day, Miss
Dismont wore an enormous kangaroo brooch that
positively sparkled with red and green gems. The
kangaroo's pouch was filled with silver numerals
that spilled out of it like a set of mathematical joeys.
As enthusiastic mathematicians, Smashie and Dontel
loved Miss Dismont's brooch. In fact, although she

loved Ms Early, Smashie sometimes wished she could visit Miss Dismont's maths class to see her and her kangaroo in action.

But of course Miss Dismont was not wearing the brooch now. She kept it in her desk and only took it out when it was time for maths.

"All these people out with the flu are going to kick themselves for missing this opportunity – I mean, this assembly," said Mr Carper. "That virus is really ripping through this place." His lip curled a bit at the sight of the students waiting to enter the building. "Doesn't help to have all these children around, does it? Germy, sticky little things."

Miss Dismont looked at him askance. "The rest of us are pretty fond of them, actually."

"Whatever. At least having so many teachers sick keeps me in business. I had Early's little fiends yesterday—"

"Please not again, please not again," John muttered.

"And today I'm in for Bean in the Infants."

"Slap my hand with your hand, my friend," said John, and he and Dontel slapped hands.

"It is too bad for the Infants, though," Smashie said.

"I can't say I'm looking forward to it," Mr Carper went on. Miss Dismont edged away. "Infants, ugh. They're even shorter and stickier than the rest of them. Still," he added with elaborate casualness, "I suppose a lot of the day will be taken up with the assembly?"

"Not for infants, Mr Carper," Miss Dismont told him. "They only come to school for a half day. They go home at a quarter past twelve."

"What!" cried Mr Carper. Then he cleared his throat and smiled at Miss Dismont. "I suppose," he said, giving a little laugh, "that no one would mind if I stuck around for the show, anyway. I'm quite a fan of nutrition—"

Miss Dismont raised her eyebrows.

"And, to be honest with you, Miss D, Mrs True is rather a … good friend of mine."

"I'm sure it would be fine, Mr Carper," said Miss Dismont, eyeing him. "If you're a fan of nutrition."

"You know what's funny?" Mr Carper asked. "I'm sure you noticed that I'm wearing a red cardigan today. I know, I know, red suits me, blah, blah. But what's crazy is that I wore a red sweater the day I posed for my dental ad, too! Can you believe?"

"Who'd've thought," said Miss Dismont.

"I know, right? I mean, I never put it together. I wonder if Mrs True will notice." He chuckled and shook his head. Then his face grew set. "Well, I'll make sure she does. I'm ready to star in that circular."

"Circular?"

"Don't tell me you aren't gunning for it, too. You all are. But it's my time, Miss Dismont. I can feel it."

"Can you," said Miss Dismont. "You'd better ring the bell now, Mr Carper. It's time for us to go in."

"Fan of nutrition," said John disgustedly. "What does he take us for?"

"Yay! Ms Early is back!"

"We missed you, Ms Early!"

"It's been crazy in here!"

"I missed you, too, Room 11," said Ms Early. "I'm so glad to see you."

Tall and elegant, Ms Early was Smashie and Dontel's favourite teacher of all the teachers they had ever had. She had a tremendous amount of style and wore clothes that draped and whooshed as she moved about the room. But the best thing about Ms Early was that she loved thinking as much as Smashie and Dontel did, and she believed firmly that all children should be encouraged and expected to think the best thoughts they could.

"We have a lot to do," she said now, standing before the class, "and I'd like us to have a good productive day of work. However—" she looked firmly at the children—"I know from Mrs Armstrong that yesterday was less than perfect."

"It's Billy's fault!"

"He's gluing people!"

"Yeah!"

"Yeah!"

"I am not!"

Ms Early held up her hand.

"No accusations," she said. "That creates an atmosphere of suspicion and then no one can do his or her best work."

The children cast their eyes down.

"And in addition to the gluing," said Ms Early, "I

was very sad to hear about Patches's disappearance. I know you are all upset about that as well."

The class nodded.

"Except for Smashie," said Joyce.

"I *am too* upset!" cried Smashie.

"I'm sure you are," said Ms Early.

"When I find out who took him—" said John.

"I'm sure no one took him, John," said Ms Early. "I'm sure he just got out somehow. Some defect in the cage door, perhaps. We must all keep our eyes out for him today."

"But Smashie told us he had to have been stolen, Ms Early," said Jacinda.

Ms Early looked at Smashie.

Smashie swallowed. "I might be wrong about that," she said, uncomfortable with the fib but mindful of not blowing their cover as investigators. Her voice was rather strangled.

"That's not what you said yesterday," said Charlene.

"Yeah," said Cyrus. "You went on and on about how Patches had no thumbs."

"Well, I think Smashie is right," said Alonso.

Smashie cast him a grateful look. "I think Patches was stolen!"

"So do I," said Charlene.

"Me too!" said Siggie. "I was going to bring my guinea pig in to show the class, but I'm not now."

"I don't blame you," said Willette.

"It's awful to know that something bad could happen any minute in Room 11!" cried Joyce. "We could be glued or … or … hamstered … or worse!"

"Children," said Ms Early, "this is exactly what I mean by creating a culture of suspicion and blame. Why, we've worked all year so far to make a wonderful community. Let's not spoil that now with false accusations and worry."

The children subsided, although they still eyed one another uneasily.

"Sorry, Ms Early."

"You're right, Ms Early."

Smashie and Dontel exchanged glances.

"We had better solve this case soon," muttered Dontel. "Before Room 11 is messed up forever."

"And I must say, I am dismayed and disappointed at your behaviour yesterday," Ms Early continued.

"I like to think my students are well behaved and focused on learning, whether I am with them or not. Mrs Armstrong will be in before morning break to discuss things further, and together we will discuss consequences for Room 11."

John coughed and counted. Once again, five children turned wide, staring eyes on Billy, who, if anything, looked even paler and more ill than he had the day before.

"Howsomever," Ms Early continued, looking in puzzlement at the starers, "you know I do not believe in holding grudges. So I think we should all put the whole situation to one side until Mrs Armstrong comes to meet with us."

"I think that's a great idea, Ms Early," said Jacinda.

"We will focus on our work," said Ms Early. "And those of you who are staring, cut it out this minute, please."

The starers stopped.

"Grr," said John.

"Good hard work," said Ms Early robustly. "That will get us back to normal. Where are my year four scientists?"

"Right here, Ms Early!" the children cried.

"Excellent," said Ms Early. "Then let's start building our pinhole cameras!"

"Hooray!"

"You'll work in pairs and help each other make your cameras. Cyrus, please pass out the instructions. Alonso, please distribute the yogurt pots."

The children leaped to get ready.

Ms Early appeared at Smashie's elbow. "Smashie," said Ms Early in a low voice, "what kind of suit is that?"

"Well," said Smashie, looking at her feet, "it is kind of a complicated suit. To help me think."

"I see," said Ms Early. She raised her eyebrows slightly but said nothing more.

"I feel terrible," Smashie whispered to Dontel. "I feel like I am fibbing! And I think Ms Early might be on to us."

"I don't think she is," said Dontel. "But I think she is worried that you might have plans."

"Well, I do," said Smashie.

Alonso came by their table with the box of yogurt pots. "Thanks, Alonso," said Dontel. He took the containers with his and Smashie's names as them.

"No, thank *you* for helping me get unstuck yesterday," said Alonso earnestly. His hand, recovered from the gluing and Smashie's and Dontel's vigorous scrubbing, still looked a little raw. "That Billy!"

It was clear that despite Ms Early's words, many still shared Alonso's sentiments. Over at his table, the kids were all paired up for work except Billy, who sat alone, twirling his pencil unhappily over his page of instructions.

"He looks like he feels pretty bad," said Dontel.

"Well, I haven't heard him say sorry," said Alonso grimly. "He's got to learn when he's taken his pranks too far!"

"Yes," said Dontel, "but I kind of think he's telling the truth when he says it wasn't him."

"Tchah," said Alonso.

The door to the classroom swung open.

"Hello, kids." It was Miss Dismont. She smiled across the room at Ms Early. "Glad to see you're back on your feet," she said.

"Thanks." Ms Early smiled. "Me too."

"Are your students in gym, Miss Dismont?" Smashie asked.

"They certainly are," said Miss Dismont. "I'm getting the room ready for our maths explorations. And after that we're starting our lesson on cartography! I'm very excited."

"I'll bet," said Cyrus.

"Aren't you going to wear your kangaroo brooch for maths, Miss Dismont?" asked Smashie. "You always do."

"Well, I want to, Smashie," said Miss Dismont. "That's why I'm here. Ms Early, you haven't seen my brooch, have you? I've looked all over this morning and can't put my hands on it. I'm heartbroken. My brother gave that to me for Christmas years ago."

"I haven't seen it," said Ms Early. "But don't worry. It'll turn up. Things always do."

"That's true, Miss Dismont," said Smashie fervently. "I lose things most every day and I almost always find them again."

"Thanks, Smashie," said Miss Dismont. "I'll hold out hope. I'm sure it got into one of my schoolbags. Well, I'd better be off to pick up my class. And I'll be by after lunch to borrow that map, Ms Early, if that's all right."

"Of course," said Ms Early.

"Thank you. Goodbye, Room 11!"

"Goodbye, Miss Dismont!"

"Ms Early!" said Jacinda. "It's just like Joyce said! Now Miss Dismont's brooch has been stolen!"

"Yeah!"

"Yeah!"

"Children!" Ms Early's voice was sharp. "You are jumping to silly conclusions and I will not have it. What happened to using your heads? Are you going to think there is a thief in our midst every time a pencil goes missing?"

"No, Ms Early."

"No, Ms Early."

"Then settle back to work. My heavens."

The children cut and measured and snipped, but some of them were still muttering.

"What are you doing with that glue, Charlene?"

"Gluing my camera! What do you think?"

"Just asking."

"Well, stop!"

"Dontel," whispered Smashie, "we have got to get going with investigating. Nobody trusts anybody anymore!"

"I know. It's awful in here!" Dontel looked at their classmates, who were milling about the room alone or in pairs, eyeing one another mistrustfully. Dontel turned to Smashie. His voice was grave. "We are going to have to do the best thinking we have ever done."

"Willette," Ms Early raised her voice slightly, her eagle eye peeled, "why aren't you working on your camera?"

"I can't get started, Ms Early. My yogurt pot wasn't in the box."

"Oh, Willette, how awful!"

Willette shrugged. "It's okay."

Ms Early addressed the class. "Did anyone get Willette's pot by mistake?"

Nobody had.

"You can have mine!" Billy jumped up and ran over to Willette, his own pot outstretched. "Here! Go ahead and take it. We have lots of empty ones at home. I'll bring in another one tomorrow."

"Billy!" said Ms Early, pleased. "That is very kind of you."

"No problem, Ms Early. I'm glad to help." Indeed, Billy looked almost sick with eagerness.

"He's trying to make people not so mad at him," Smashie whispered to Dontel. She understood the impulse.

"I think you're right."

"I could help Willette make her camera now," said Billy earnestly to Ms Early, "and then I'll work on mine at home by myself after school. That way both of us will be all caught up for tomorrow."

"I don't want to work with Billy," Willette said instantly.

"Willette Williams, that is not the way we approach teamwork in Room 11." Ms Early was stern.

"But I don't want to be glued!"

"I'm telling you!" cried Billy. "For the last time, it wasn't me!"

"Hello, hello!" The busy door of Room 11 whizzed open once more and a set of blond curls appeared, beaming, inside it.

It was Mr Carper.

CHAPTER 18
Alibis

"Oh." Clutching a large plastic pork chop in one hand, Mr Carper started at the sight of the children. "They're here. I thought they had art first thing." He gestured in the direction of the art room with the chop.

"Why does he have a pork chop?" Smashie whispered puzzledly to Dontel.

"Probably he's practicing with it," Dontel whispered back. "For that circular."

"I bet you're right," said Smashie. "And I bet he got it from the Infants' pretend grocery store."

"Room 11 only has art on Tuesdays," said Ms Early, eyeing the chop. "Is there something I can help you with?"

Mr Carper hesitated, then flashed his teeth in a disarmingly wide smile.

"Oh, I think you can, Ms Early," he said with a throaty chuckle.

"In what way?" said Ms Early, her eye growing chilly.

"Just thought I'd pop in and see if you were free. See if you wanted to talk over how things went when you were out, blah and blah."

"Why don't you show her those packets?" Dontel muttered. "She'll be real glad about those."

"I'm afraid we're rather busy just now," said Ms Early.

"Well, when are you free? Don't the kids have library time or something?"

"I thought he liked Mrs True," whispered Jacinda.

"I think he thinks Mrs True likes *him*," said Joyce.

"Ugh," said Smashie.

"No library today," said Ms Early. "We have the nutrition assembly this afternoon instead."

Mr Carper's lips twisted. Then, straightening, he reapplied his smile. "So disappointing," he said with a rueful chuckle. "I was looking forward to visiting with you right away. You know, Ms Early – wait, what's your first name?"

"Let's stick with Ms Early."

"Ha-ha, that's right, don't want to confuse the kiddies, hey?" Mr Carper grinned at her and waggled his eyebrows.

Dontel clapped his hand to his forehead and shook his head from side to side.

"How come he cares so much about her name?" Smashie whispered to Dontel. "Why doesn't he just call her Teacher with the Head or something, like he does with the rest of us?"

"Anyway," Mr Carper continued, "funny thing about that assembly, *Ms Early*. Huge coincidence. I mean, I model, right, and here's the True Yum *looking* for a model, and they show up here on the exact day I'm substituting!"

"Mr Carper, aren't you expected down in the Infants?"

"Oh, the aide is taking over. What do I know about

infants? Well, anyway, all I'm saying is that I think someone might be making an appearance soon in a grocery store near you, if you know what I mean."

"I really don't."

"The circular," said much of Room 11.

"Spot on, kiddies," said Mr Carper. He held the pork chop to his mouth and made as if to take a large bite. His teeth gleamed as he held the pose.

"Oh," said Ms Early. "Yes. Miss Dismont mentioned you were ... interested in that."

"Yes." Mr Carper smiled. "I'm something of a—"

"Frontunner," Charlene finished wearily.

Mr Carper glared at her. "Yes, Girl in the T-Shirt," he said. "I am."

"So kind of you to drop by," Ms Early said. But Mr Carper did not take the hint. He glanced toward the back of the room and nodded at Patches's empty cage.

"What about that hamster?" he asked. "Did anyone find it?"

"Not yet," said Ms Early. "But we are holding out hope."

Mr Carper snorted. "Yeah, right," he said. "Are

you going to keep that cage in the back of the room? Because those things are full of —"

"Indeed we are, Mr Carper," said Ms Early crisply. "Now, if you'll excuse us, we need to get back to our cameras, and I am quite sure you need to get back to the Infants." She glanced at the pork chop. "And return their materials."

Mr Carper chuckled. "All right, I get it. I'll wait until we can be alone," he said. He glanced again at the back of the room. "I'll grab that cage for you if you want," he said. "Clean it out, get rid of all the —"

"Smooth, man," John muttered. "Because that's what all the ladies want, a clean hamster cage."

"Better than flowers," Siggie murmured back, and the two boys laughed.

"Goodbye, Mr Carper," Ms Early said firmly.

"Ta-ta," said Mr Carper, and, knotting his cardigan casually around his neck, at last he went.

"Let me measure our yogurt pots," Smashie said as she and Dontel got back to work on their cameras.

"Sure," said Dontel. "And after you do that," he muttered, "let's do some investigating. See who remembers whom being where when."

Smashie looked at him admiringly. "That was a wonderful sentence," she said.

Dontel smiled shyly. "Thank you," he said. "I thought of it last night. Anyway, we should start questioning people."

"Yes," Smashie agreed. "Ask them if they saw anything strange."

"But we have to do it without arousing suspicion."

"Exactly."

Dontel turned to Jacinda.

"Jacinda," he said casually, "who all did you eat lunch with yesterday?"

"Who wants to know?" Jacinda asked amiably, cutting out a square of aluminum foil.

"Just wondering," said Dontel. "I'm trying to, uh, develop my memory. See if I can remember exact details of things. I'm, uh, working on remembering everything about the lunchroom yesterday."

"Huh," said Jacinda. "Well, whatever floats your boat, I guess. I sat with Tatiana, Charlene, and Joyce. Like every other day."

"That's right," said Dontel. "I remember now."

Smashie sidled away and over to Cyrus.

"Wasn't lunchtime just the worst yesterday?" she asked him offhandedly. "Didn't the people you hung out with think it stunk, not to get to play? Who *did* you hang out with, there on the playground?"

"I read to the year two classes with Willette, remember? I barely had any time out on the playground."

"Oh. That's right." She narrowed her eyes at him. "So you were with the year twos for the whole entire time until you came back out to the playground?"

"What are you, a detective? Of course I was. Ask their teacher, Ms Dart." Cyrus snipped and glued.

Smashie smiled hastily. "Of course I am not a detective," she said. "You didn't think this was a Detective Suit, did you?"

Cyrus glanced at her outfit. "No," he said. "I don't really get what kind of suit that is."

"It is just my clothes today, Cyrus, is all."

"I see," said Cyrus.

"Smashie," Ms Early called, "why aren't you at your own seat?"

"I'm going, Ms Early," said Smashie, and sidled hastily back to her table. "It is very hard to question people closely about their movements without making them suspicious," she whispered to Dontel.

"Or without making them think you're strange," Dontel agreed.

"I think we're ready to paint, Ms Early," said Jacinda.

Ms Early passed a weary hand over her brow. "I think we'll save that until later, Jacinda. We've had a lot of interruptions this morning, and this is taking longer than I thought it would. Let's move on to reading now. We'll finish our cameras after morning break."

Ensconced in the cushions in the reading area, Smashie and Dontel hastily read the chapter in the novel Ms Early had assigned and moved on to their investigation.

"Let's write down all the people who have alibis," said Smashie, pulling her Investigation Notebook and a pencil out of one of her pouches. "Which is also good Investigator Language."

"Good idea," said Dontel. "It is."

PEOPLE WITH ALIBIS
Billy
Mr Carper
John
Jacinda
Tatiana
Joyce
Charlene

"And Cyrus," said Smashie. "Add him and Willette. I am kind of terrible at investigating, Dontel. I forgot I even saw those two coming back from reading to the year two classes when I ran back for my hoodie. What kind of investigator forgets things like that?"

"Well, we are only beginners," said Dontel. "We will get less terrible. Eight kids down and eleven to go." He sighed. "We sure have our work cut out for us."

"Let's think about the other idea I had yesterday at your house," said Smashie.

"Not the mad scientist again," moaned Dontel.

"No. Though that was an excellent idea," said Smashie. "See here; if you don't want to listen to what I—"

"I'm sorry, Smash," said Dontel. "I didn't mean it was a bad idea. But what did you really mean just now?"

"I meant my idea about if anyone was wearing suspicious clothes yesterday."

"I remember," said Dontel. "You wanted to investigate if anybody was wearing an all-black Thief Suit."

"Yes," said Smashie. "Or if somebody was in a mask."

"But, Smashie, I think we all would have noticed if someone had been wearing anything like that."

"Not necessarily!" said Smashie. "Not if it were something that was a part of a person's regular clothes!"

"What do you mean?" Dontel furrowed his brow.

"I mean," said Smashie, leaning forward, "Alonso Day!"

"Alonso? What?"

"That balaclava hat!" Smashie cried. "Think about it! Nobody would recognize him if he had that on! He could sneak in anywhere and steal any number of hamsters! I am entering his name on the Suspect List right now," she said, and set to purposefully with her pencil.

SUSPECT LIST
1. ~~Billy Kamarski~~
2. ~~Mr Carper~~
3. ~~Me~~
4. Alonso Day

"Except," said Dontel, "that he is the only one in the whole school that wears that kind of hat, so if he wore it inside to steal hamsters, everybody would know it was him. It would be a terrible disguise, Smashie."

Smashie blinked.

"Also, he was with our class the whole time during lunch. That was when he got glued." Dontel cleared his throat. "To, uh, that balaclava hat."

Smashie's shoulders slumped. "Rats." She blinked at her Investigation Notebook. Then she took up her pencil once more.

PEOPLE TO CLEAR ALONSO'S NAME: Us.

And she crossed out Alonso's name.

"Dontel," she said. "I do not think we will ever solve this case."

"Think of it this way," said Dontel. "At least we're narrowing down the list of suspects."

"That is a good point," said Smashie.

"I wouldn't mind if someone ran by and shouted the name of the thief at us, though," said Dontel.

"The way it happens for that detective in my grand-ma's books."

"That would be nice," said Smashie. "But we will be prouder if we use our own brains."

"Clean up, children," called Ms Early. "It's time for—"

BAM!

CHAPTER 19

Clues and Confiscation

Why doesn't Mrs Armstrong ever open the door gently?
Smashie wondered.

The moment of reckoning had come. Mrs
Armstrong had arrived, and she and Ms Early were
ready to address the class about the consequences of
people gluing people to things.

"Good morning, Ms Early," said Mrs Armstrong.

"Good morning, Mrs Armstrong." Ms Early went
to the front of the class and stood beside the indignant

headmistress. "Children, please give us your full attention. You know what this conversation is about."

"Ms Early and I are both ILL about this whole gluing fiasco!" Mrs Armstrong exclaimed.

"Completely unacceptable behaviour," Ms Early agreed. "We are very disappointed."

"We've discussed the matter thoroughly," Mrs Armstrong continued, "and have agreed that we will continue with silent indoor morning break and no-games lunch break until someone comes forward."

"Oh, no!" cried Charlene.

Ms Early held up her hand. "Room 11 is a team," she said. "And one member of our team has violated the trust of the rest of the team. Now, I have every faith that that person is sorry and knows how to do the right thing. I am sure that person will not permit the whole class to suffer. Therefore, I agree with Mrs Armstrong and we will carry on as she has said regarding free time until that person comes forward. I feel confident it will not be long."

"Grr," said John, but not loud enough for her to hear. "I feel confident it better not be long, or I'll—"

"In addition," said Mrs Armstrong, "until you can

prove yourselves responsible with gluing materials, all gluing privileges are hereby suspended."

Room 11 gasped. "*All* gluing privileges?" they cried.

"All of them, I am afraid." Ms Early nodded. "The gluer has shown that he or she cannot control his or her impulses to glue. Therefore, although I know several of you still need to glue portions of your cameras, all the gluing materials in the room are being confiscated immediately. That includes glue sticks, squeezable bottles, rubber cement, and, of course, the hot-glue guns."

"Mr Bloom will keep the materials for you in his office until you earn them back." Mrs Armstrong shook her head in despair. "I hope you know we never wanted it to come to this, Room 11! We are ill at the stomach with a basin beside the bed about the whole situation!"

And she left, closing the door firmly behind her.

"Man," said Alonso.

"Heck," said Smashie.

"Let's get this over with." Ms Early sighed. "One of you can bring the things to Mr Bloom right now."

"I'll go!" cried Jacinda.

"I will!"

"I will!"

All of the children were eager for a chance to visit with the kindly caretaker.

"I'll use the name tin so it will be fair," said Ms Early. The name tin was an old biscuit container filled with small plastic chips, each of which had the name of a member of Room 11 written on it.

Ms Early averted her gaze and plunged her hand in the tin. "Dontel Marquise," she read from the chip.

Dontel beamed.

"Lucky!" said Smashie.

"I'll gather the things up right now," he said, and went to the supplies area. "Ms Early?" he called after a moment, his arms overflowing with materials he had gathered. "There's too much here for just me. Could I please have help?"

"Gracious," said Ms Early. "Who would have thought we had so many gluing materials? All right. Smashie, help your friend, please."

Hooray!

Smashie leaped to obey.

★ ★ ★

Smashie and Dontel headed out the side door of the Rebecca Lee Crumpler Primary School and stepped onto the little path that led behind the building to Mr Bloom's office. They could already hear his music playing – opera ladies, from the sound of it.

"Dontel," said Smashie as they picked their way carefully down the path, "this is a terrific opportunity."

"I know," said Dontel. "Me and Mr Bloom can talk about space."

"Yes," said Smashie. "But also we can question him! See if he noticed any of our classmates carrying out suspicious activity in our room during lunch!"

"I am starting to worry that maybe it wasn't a member of our class at all, Smash," said Dontel. "We have got to be open to that possibility."

It was a dreadful one. There were plenty of other students in the Rebecca Lee Crumpler Primary school, not to mention families and guests popping in the whole time. If they had to include all of those people, this investigation might get kind of exhausting.

"Well," said Smashie, resolute, "Mr Bloom

knows everyone and everything that goes on in this school. He just might know something that can help us."

They arrived at Mr Bloom's office. Smashie's hands were so full of glue that she had to knock on the door with her elbow.

The door flew open.

"Sous le dôme épais où le blanc jasmin…" sang the opera ladies Frenchly.

"Why, if it isn't little Miss McP and Mr M!" Mr Bloom beamed. "Come in, come in. Been expecting someone from your class. Mrs A told me to be on the lookout."

He peered at them over his spectacles.

"I guess you heard about the glue," said Smashie.

"Yuss," said Mr Bloom. "I did. What's the matter with you kids? Don't you know you ain't supposed to glue folks to things?"

"Me and Smashie do," said Dontel. "It's just one person in our class that doesn't."

"Hrrmm," said Mr Bloom. "Well, pile those things over there on the table by the winda. But don't get none of that sticky stuff on my telescope."

"We'll be careful, Mr Bloom."

"Heard you kids lost that hamster, too," Mr Bloom said. "Now, that's too bad. Nice little fellas, hamsters. One at a time, that is. Put two of them together, now, and that's a whole different ball of wax. Some fight to see."

"Mr Bloom," said Smashie, "you didn't see anybody in our room at lunchtime, did you?"

"No, sirree," said the caretaker. "But I waren't over by your room during your lunch, Miss McP. I was over to the year sixes, remember? They have science when you all are having lunch, and I was special guest lecturer for their science class. Astronomy."

"Oh," said Smashie. "That's right."

"We forgot," said Dontel.

They were crestfallen.

"Mighty smart group of youngsters in there," said Mr Bloom.

"Did the lecture go well, Mr Bloom?" Smashie asked politely.

"It surely did. I simulated a spaceflight for them. Got all the way through Mach Three!"

"Man!" said Dontel. "I wish I could have been there!"

"Well, next time, I'll send someone over to you with an invite."

"Thank you, Mr Bloom!"

"Me too, Mr Bloom?" asked Smashie.

"Sure thing. Now, kids, I been saving my back

issues of *Sky and Telescope* for your class. Don't have no more use for them. Would you all like to take them to Room 11 to peruse?"

"Gosh, Mr Bloom," said Dontel. "That would be great."

"Swell," said Mr Bloom. "Let me load you up. Twenty apiece," he said, placing the magazines across their outstretched arms. "There. That ought to last you."

Smashie and Dontel staggered back out the door and onto the path.

"Too bad Mr Bloom didn't have any useful information for our investigation," said Dontel.

"Yes," said Smashie. "But it is very nice that he gave us all these magazines."

"It sure is," Dontel agreed. "But it would be even nicer if we could narrow the field of suspects a little bit. Or find some kind of clue."

"We could start a new list in our Investigation Notebooks," said Smashie. "People Who Could Have Helped Us by Seeing a Suspect Enter the Room but Were Somewhere Else Instead so They Didn't See Anyone. Then we could put, *Number 1: Mr Bloom*."

"I don't have my Investigation Notebook with me," Dontel admitted. "Too big for my pocket. Otherwise we could both write that down right now. Only maybe a little bit more concisely."

"I have my notebook right here, in one of my macramé pouches," said Smashie smugly. "You should have worn the sash I made you, Dontel. It would be so handy. I don't understand why Mr Carper won't put things in his pockets, do you? The more pockets the better is what I say!"

She emphasized her words with a proud gesture toward her sash, which turned out to be a mistake, because she lost her grip on her magazines and all twenty of them tumbled to the ground.

"Yeeps!" cried Smashie as the magazines flipped and slipped down the path.

"Yeeps!" Dontel agreed. He laid down his own armful of magazines and helped Smashie gather the ones that had skittered away.

"Ugh," Smashie said. "I've only got nineteen. One is still missing."

"Don't worry," said Dontel reassuringly. "We'll find it."

"I hope so," said Smashie. Then, stooping over, she peered and poked and gathered her way along the path until she found herself at the back of Mr Bloom's office.

What she saw there made her gasp.

"Dontel!" she shouted.

"What is it, Smash? Did you find the last one?"

"No!" Smashie cried. "But come quick! I think I have found an Important Clue!"

CHAPTER 20
Deducing!

"What did you find, Smash?"

"This!" Smashie pointed at the edge of ground abutting Mr Bloom's office. Dontel squatted down beside her.

Pressed into the soft muddy dirt were two shallow depressions. The first was a cylindrical imprint, some ten centimetres across its circular base and a few centimetres deep. The second was about twice as long as the first, nearly rectangular in outline, but curving softly into the soil. The ground beside these imprints was littered with little green pellets.

"I don't know what those dents are," said Dontel, "but that green stuff is hamster food!"

"Exactly!" said Smashie. "And look – wood shavings, too!"

It was true. Shavings were scattered all over the dirt nearby.

"And that means Patches!" cried Dontel.

"Yes!" cried Smashie. "Patches was here!"

"Smashie," said Dontel, "you have got a really good eye."

"Thank you," said Smashie. "It is because I finally feel like an Investigator, I think. My suit is helping."

"But—" Dontel swallowed. "Smashie, you don't think it was Mr Bloom who took Patches, do you?"

"No," said Smashie. "I don't."

Dontel sighed with relief. "Phew," he said. "Because I really like Mr Bloom."

"Me too," said Smashie. "But it wasn't him. In fact, I am positive that the thief is a member of our own class!"

"You are? How come? Any old body could have gotten Patches some shavings and some food."

"That is true," said Smashie. "But not everybody would have had ready access to a yogurt pot to smuggle him away in!"

"A yogurt pot!"

"Yes!" cried Smashie. "I am sure of it! Just look at these dents in the dirt! They are exactly the right size. This one with the circular base is where the thief stood the pot up at first, with Patches inside.

Then he or she must have changed his or her mind and laid the pot down sideways so Patches would have more room to move around. That's what made this longer dent!"

"Smashie," said Dontel, "I think you are kind of a genius."

"Well," said Smashie fairly, "we have spent a lot of time with those yogurt pots."

"So the thief smuggled Patches away at lunchtime and brought him here?"

"Yes," said Smashie. "I hope he or she made air-holes in the container."

"I'll bet he or she did," said Dontel. "If the thief took the trouble to bring shavings and food for him, it only makes sense that he or she would have made airholes for him, too."

"That is true," said Smashie. "Dontel, this was a very well-thought-out plan. Hiding Patches here was very smart of the thief."

"I guess," said Dontel. "In a bad, robber sort of way."

"That is what I mean. It was thief-smart. The person knew that Mr Bloom wouldn't be here at lunchtime because of his lecture. Mr Carper read about it to us in the morning announcements."

"So the thief was sure that no one would be here to find Patches."

"Yes," said Smashie. "And everybody knows that Mr Bloom plays his music extra loud whenever he *is* in here, so he wouldn't have heard Patches go *scrabble, scrabble, scrabble* even when he *was* back in his office!"

"And plus it would have been easy for the thief to come grab Patches in his container at the end of the day and sneak him away in his or her backpack."

"Yes," Smashie agreed. "Now all we have to do is ask people about where they were at the end of the day yesterday. We need to find out if anybody slipped out of the line when Mr Carper brought us out to the buses. You could pretend you are strengthening your memory again, Dontel—"

But Dontel was shaking his head.

"We don't have to do that, Smashie," he said. "I know who the thief is!"

CHAPTER 21

The Perp?

"Willette Williams," said Dontel.

"Willette?"

"Willette. Think about it. Who was missing her yogurt pot this morning?"

"Willette!"

"Right! And she didn't seem any too upset about it."

"Well, she doesn't really like making things."

"But that just proves it! She *extra* wouldn't mind using up her yogurt pot to steal Patches because she wouldn't care if she wasn't able to make her camera!"

"*You* are the genius, Dontel!" cried Smashie. "Plus Willette gets picked up after school by her babysitter—"

"So it would be easy for her to steal away to fetch Patches at the end of the day. That's it, Smashie! I am sure we are right this time!"

"Dontel," said Smashie, "we are getting very excellent at being investigators."

"We sort of are, aren't we?"

They beamed proudly at each other.

Then Smashie's eyes widened. "Does this mean," she asked, "that Willette is a mad scientist who wants to switch brains with Patches?"

"Heck, no," said Dontel. "Only, I can't think of a reason why she *would* steal him, either. The other motives we thought of don't really fit."

"That is true," said Smashie. "Willette is not the joke-playing type, and she is also not mean. Unless she is mad at a person for something," she added, remembering Willette's stony glares at her during the class pet discussions.

"And she also sure doesn't hate Patches," said Dontel.

"Wait!" cried Smashie. "That's it!"

"What do you mean?"

"Dontel," said Smashie, "who would be happy that Patches was missing?"

"You," said Dontel. "And Mr Carper."

"Grr," said Smashie. "You are just like the rest of them. What I mean is, who would be very glad if Patches were to be gone from Room 11?"

"I don't know," said Dontel. "Who?"

"A person who had stolen him *to be her very own hamster!*"

"Smashie!"

"To live in her very own house forever! To cuddle whenever she wanted!"

"That's it, Smashie!" Dontel's eyes were flashing. "That makes perfect sense! All of us in Room 11 love Patches—"

"Except for me—"

"Except for you. But Willette—"

Their eyes met. Smashie nodded. They finished the sentence together: "Loves him almost Too Much!"

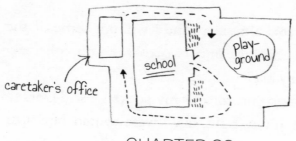

CHAPTER 22

Taxing Someone with the Crime

"I can't believe I fell for her old 'reading to the year twos' alibi!" said Smashie. "Why, it would have been simple for her to sneak out a few minutes early, steal Patches, hide him here, and then run back to the year two area in time to meet Cyrus and go out to the playground!"

"That is exactly what must have happened," Dontel agreed. "Let's draw a picture of the crime scene in your Investigation Notebook. Just so we can spell it out for everybody."

"Yes," said Smashie. "And I will put some of the feed and shavings into two of the clue-collecting spots in my hat."

"I'll take some, too, for my pockets," said Dontel. "I'm sure you're right, but I want to compare it to what we have in Room 11. Just to make sure. That's the scientific method."

Smashie lowered her eyebrows and her voice grew grim. "That's fine. But first we go in and tax Willette with her crimes." But her serious manner broke as she spoke. "That's a good phrase. I'm putting that on the Investigator Language page, too." And flipping to the back of her notebook, she added it to the list:

INVESTIGATOR LANGUAGE
1. Suspect
2. Detective
3. Investigate
4. Motive
5. Exonerate
6. Access
7. Tax someone with their crimes

"Good," said Dontel. "And now we draw." They huddled over Smashie's notebook and began to sketch the scene of the crime.

Smashie and Dontel marched purposefully forth, arms full of magazines and hearts focused on justice. Their knees spiked in tandem down the hallway to Room 11.

They burst into the room.

"Willette Williams!" Smashie cried. "Where were you yesterday at lunch?"

"Don't even bother to answer, Willette, because we already know!" Dontel joined in. "Look at this sketch!"

"Dontel and Smashie." Ms Early's voice was incredulous. "What is the *matter* with you? Is that how we enter a room?"

"What is the matter with us is Patches, Ms Early!" Smashie cried. She turned to face her class-mates. "We accuse Willette Williams of the theft of Patches!"

"What!" shouted Willette.

"What are you talking about?" exclaimed Jacinda.

"Willette?" said Siggie. "Never!"

The class was aghast. So was Ms Early. "Smashie McPepper," she began warningly, but Smashie was on a roll.

"Were you really reading to the year twos, Willette?" she asked. "Or were you stealing into the classroom to take Patches home to be your very own?"

Willette burst into tears.

"I would never steal Patches! I love him too much to frighten him like that! I'd never take him away from the only home he's ever known," she sobbed. "Waah-aah-aaaah!"

"A likely story," said Dontel over Willette's wails.

Ms Early put her arm around Willette. "Smashie and Dontel, I don't know what you are up to," she said. "But in this class, we *do not* accuse our friends of something unless we have proof! Didn't you listen to a word I said this morning?"

"But we do have proof!" cried Smashie.

"Well, it would have to be proof that Willette is magic," said Charlene unexpectedly. "Or that she has a secret twin. Because my sister is in first grade and all she talked about after school was how great Willette was when she read to them. In fact, my sister was allowed to walk with Willette over to the other first grade to pick up Cyrus when the reading time was over. So, unless you're saying that Cyrus was in on it, too—"

Cyrus scowled. "Yeah, just try saying that—"

"Then the two of you owe Willette an apology!"

And Charlene, too, put an arm around her crying friend.

"Just ask Mr Chu in the first grade." Willette gulped. "I was never out of his room for an instant." She flung her head back and redoubled her sobs. "Waaaahhhhh! WAAHHHHH!"

Her mouth was a trapezoid. The class could see right down to her tonsils. They turned accusing, angry eyes on Smashie and Dontel.

Smashie and Dontel swallowed.

"I guess we were wrong," said Smashie.

"We're awfully sorry, Willette," said Dontel.

"This is exactly what I mean by the consequences of getting carried away," said Ms Early.

"You're right," said Dontel sadly. "I knew the proper scientific method would be to wait and compare the feed samples we found to the ones we have in here and then check to see if Willette had any on her person, but I was too excited."

"It's my fault," said Smashie. "I infected you with my hecticness."

Ms Early held up her hand to hush them. "It's both of your faults. I know you are sad about Patches—"

"Smashie's not," said John.

Smashie grimaced.

"But you have to think before you speak. Smashie, we've been working on that all year. And Dontel—" Ms Early shook her head—"you're usually one of the most level-headed children in the class. I don't know what has gotten into you."

Smashie's and Dontel's faces burned like fire. They blinked and looked shamefacedly at their shoes.

"We owe the whole class an apology," said Dontel. "We're sorry, everybody."

"Truly," said Smashie. "Willette, I've got a cupcake in my lunch. You can have it."

"Smashie has one for me, too, Willette, and it's all yours as well," said Dontel.

Willette sniffed and gulped. "What kind are they?" she asked.

"Chocolate," said Smashie. "With iced robots on top."

"Cupcakes are a start," said Ms Early. "In addition, you two will do Willette's end-of-the-day classroom clean-up job for the rest of the week, as well as your own."

Smashie and Dontel nodded. "We will," said Dontel.

"We'll do it even longer if you want, Willette," said Smashie. It was no less than they deserved. Willette looked satisfied, though her eyes were still red.

"My job is sweeping," she snuffled. "And this floor gets good and dirty, too."

"Charlene, why don't you take Willette to get a drink of water," Ms Early continued. "The rest of you, take your seats. It's time for our silent morning break. I hope all of you use the time to reflect on all this and what it will take for us to become a happy, productive class once more."

"I'll reflect, all right," John muttered. "I'd like to reflect someone right in the nose."

"John," said Ms Early.

"Sorry," said John.

But it wasn't just John who was still angry. Room 11 watched coldly as Smashie and Dontel set their piles of magazines down in the science area and made their way to their table.

"Now you know how it feels," Billy muttered to them as they passed. He was still pale this morning, exhausted looking, with purple circles under his eyes.

"Poor guy," murmured Dontel.

But it was true, what Billy said. The class's anger had risen to new heights. Smashie and Dontel were now reviled every bit as much as Billy.

The collar of Smashie's repurposed hot-suit began to itch unbearably.

Ms Early looked through some of Room 11's mathematics papers at her desk while the children sat for morning break, hands folded and silent. Many of them flung occasional glares at Billy, Smashie, or Dontel.

This is the worst, thought Smashie. Dontel sat bleak-eyed beside her.

Knock, knock!

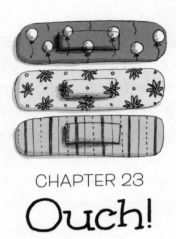

CHAPTER 23
Ouch!

Once more the active door of Room 11 was flung open. Mr Carper, as promised, was back.

"Don't you want to step along to the staffroom for a coffee?" He beamed at Ms Early. "Not very nice to sit alone in an empty—"

Then he noticed the children. He scowled.

"Oh," he said. "They're here? Shouldn't they be outside for morning break?"

"We are having a silent indoor morning break, Mr Carper," said Ms Early.

"Oh, that's right. They're being punished. Terrif."
He scowled. "Say, Ms Early," he said, flashing his
smile once more, "you still look a little peaky. Not
quite up to snuff. If you want to push along home,
I'd be glad to take over for you. Had a grand time in
here yesterday."

"What?" squawked Joyce.

"Come again?" said Alonso.

"Aren't you still with the Infants, Mr Carper?"
asked Ms Early.

"Oh, we'll smoosh your class in with them. The
aide can handle it. What you need is rest. Out of
here and home on the couch. Come on. Let's get
you packed up."

"But he hates us," said Charlene.

"Maybe he hates infants more," said Smashie to
Dontel.

"I think," said Dontel, eyeing Mr Carper, "it's
more that he likes Ms Early."

"I'm quite well, thank you, Mr Carper," said Ms
Early, her tone clipped. "And I'm afraid we'll have
to chat another time. This really is supposed to be a
silent breaktime."

"I think you should forget that," said Mr Carper. "Take them outside to run around a little in the fresh air and give the germs a chance to air out of this place."

"I'm afraid not."

"Oh, fine," said the substitute. "I'll come back at lunch."

"Shoot, man," John muttered as Mr Carper left, "have some pride."

Silent break was over, but the class's mood had not improved.

Smashie and Dontel, subdued, hunched over their pinhole cameras once more.

"We have to solve this case, Smash," said Dontel. "The whole class is furious with us."

"I know." Smashie was miserable. "I'm an awful investigator. I don't deserve to wear this Investigation Suit."

"Don't talk like that, Smashie," said Dontel. "Honest, our thinking was super. We were deducing stuff very logically. We were just wrong is all."

"How are we ever going to solve it?" Smashie was in despair. "We are back to everybody having an alibi, and we have run out of kinds of motives!"

"Maybe the perpetrator *is* a scientist," said Dontel. "Not a mad one. But maybe one who wants to study why hamsters have that kind of feet."

Smashie shuddered.

Ms Early addressed the class. "I know it will be a challenge for a few of you to finish your cameras without glue," she said. "You will have to use tape as a temporary measure." She drifted to a stop by Smashie and Dontel's table. "I'm also noticing that a few of you still need to cut the aluminum foil for the aperture. I trust you and your partner to make good decisions about who should use the scissors. For example, if you know you struggle with sharp things, you could ask your partner—"

"Take the hint, Smashie," Dontel muttered. "Pass me those clippers."

Ms Early, overhearing, nodded slightly.

Smashie's face grew stormy. "I'd like to work the scissors, please."

"Smashie—"

Smashie narrowed her eyes. "Pass me the scissors, please."

Dontel did. Smashie cut.

The inevitable ensued.

"Ms Early," Dontel called, "I think Smashie needs to go to the nurse."

"It's just a little scrape," said Smashie, showing Nurse Wattley her hurt finger. The worst of the throbbing had stopped, and there was just a small bead of blood gathering at the tip.

"That's right. A one-plasterer this time, Smashie. Pick your poison." The nurse held out the jar of plasters. Smashie chose a red one printed with balloons.

I need a cheerful plaster, she thought, *what with it being so terrible down in Room 11.*

"Yow," she said, flinching as Nurse Wattley put antiseptic on her cut and wrapped her finger. "You must be sick of my class, Nurse Wattley."

"Not really," said the nurse. "Why should I be?"

"Billy in here yesterday, me today. We're taking up a lot of your time."

"Billy Kamarski?" Nurse Wattley threw away the plaster wrapper. "He wasn't in here yesterday. I haven't had that boy in here all year."

Smashie stared at her. Then she leaped from the table.

"Thank you, Nurse Wattley!" she cried.

"My plasters are your plasters, Smashie. But don't run down the hall!"

But Smashie was too excited to walk, for, once again, she had solved the case of Patches, the missing hamster!

CHAPTER 24

Solved?

"Billy Kamarski?" Dontel whispered incredulously as Smashie arrived breathlessly back at Room 11. "*Billy* stole Patches?"

The class was cleaning up and getting ready to line up for lunch.

"Yes!" Smashie whispered back fiercely. There was no time to lose. "His alibi is a sham! He never went to the nurse yesterday at all!"

"No!"

"Yes!"

"Smashie!"

"I know!"

"He *lied*!"

"Yes!" Smashie leaped about. "It all fits, Dontel! Who was the one who was so eager to give Willette his own yogurt pot?"

"Billy!"

"Yes! And *not* because he wanted the class to think he was nice —"

"But because he used hers to smuggle out Patches!"

"Yes! And Billy walks home after school, so at the end of the day, he could have doubled back just as easy as Willette to pick Patches up from his hiding place by Mr Bloom's office."

"I'm sure you're right, Smash." But Dontel's happy grin turned to puzzlement. "Why, though? Do you think it was just a prank?"

"I suppose so," said Smashie. "Only, I keep thinking about what we were saying yesterday. He really isn't acting like he usually does after a prank."

"That's what I think, too."

"Well, maybe he got overwhelmed with this on top of the glue thing or something. I don't know why he did it," said Smashie, drawing herself up. "But I do know that, this time, we're right."

"So what'll we do?" asked Dontel.

"Tax Billy with his crimes!"

"I am a little nervous about that," Dontel admitted. "It didn't go so well when we taxed Willette."

"It will this time," said Smashie confidently. "We had better bring our Investigation Notebooks to lunch, Dontel. You can put yours in one of my pouches if you want."

The class was in the hallway, ready to file to the canteen. Miss Dismont's class was just ahead of them.

"Did you find that brooch, Miss Dismont?" asked Ms Early.

"Nope," said Miss Dismont sadly. "But we managed to have maths without it."

"I'll keep my fingers crossed for you," said Ms Early.

"Thanks."

As the two women spoke, Smashie and Dontel sidled up to Billy. Now he stood sandwiched between them in line, his lunch bag clutched in his hands.

"Hello, Billy," said Smashie darkly.

"How are you, Billy?" asked Dontel in equally dolorous tones.

"Fine." Billy licked his lips. "What's going on? Why are you two looking at me like that?"

"We'd like to sit with you today, Billy," said Smashie.

"You would?" Billy asked cautiously. "Why?"

"We just would," said Dontel.

"We think we could have a good conversation with you."

"About what?" Billy quivered. His face, already pale, grew paler still.

Smashie fixed him with a look. This was no time for sympathy. She deepened her voice. "Various things."

"Okay, Room 11," Ms Early called. "Here we go."

But before she could turn to lead the line of children to the canteen, a hand appeared over her shoulder and tapped it. Ms Early sprang into the air and whirled around.

It was Mr Carper.

"Dude," muttered John.

Ms Early wilted. "You startled me, Mr Carper," she said.

"My apologies." Mr Carper looked at the key in her hand. "You haven't locked up, have you?"

"Yes," said Ms Early. "I am through with having drama in Room 11. Nobody is getting into that room while we are out."

"Is that really necessary?" Mr Carper glanced through the window in the door to the back of the room. "Haven't all of your hamsters already been taken?"

He chuckled.

Ms Early did not.

"Hey, hey, hey," said Mr Carper, laying a hand on her arm. "Whoa. Hold up."

"Mr Carper," said Ms Early, "we are in a hurry. All right, class. File."

Mr Carper released her arm and stepped aside to let the children pass, banging his fist gently on the locked door.

Behind Smashie, Willette sniffed. "Those had better be some good cupcakes, Smashie."

"They are," Smashie promised. "I really am sorry,

Willette. With any luck, I'll have something even better than cupcakes for you by the end of lunch, too."

Smashie and Dontel herded Billy to a small table in the back of the canteen. He sat between them, facing front, while they straddled the bench on either side of him.

"We know what you did, Billy," said Smashie into his right ear.

"We have evidence and everything," said Dontel into his left. "The jig is up."

"I don't know what you're talking about." But Billy's mouth trembled as he spoke, and he crumbled a lemon square in his fingers. "Is this about the glue?" he asked hopefully.

"No," said Smashie. "This is about Patches."

The lemon square fell from Billy's fingers.

"We know you were not with Nurse Wattley at lunchtime yesterday," said Smashie.

"And we know you smuggled Patches out of Room 11 in Willette's yogurt pot."

"We even found the spot by Mr Bloom's office where you hid him until the end of the day."

Billy's shoulders sagged. "I didn't mean to take Willette's pot," he whispered. "I thought I grabbed mine."

"So you admit you are the swiper of Patches?" said Smashie.

"Yes," Billy said dully. "You got me."

"But why did you do it, Billy?" asked Dontel. "Why would you bother pulling another prank?"

"It wasn't a prank!" Billy whipped his head back and forth to look at them both. "I had to do it! Don't you see? Didn't you see the way he looked at him?"

"Who?" asked Dontel.

"Mr Carper!" Billy's voice was anguished. "He kept saying how awful Patches was! He kept saying he couldn't stand hamsters and that Patches was disgusting!"

"Well, not everybody likes hamsters, Billy," said Dontel. "Smashie here, for example—"

"*Dontel.*"

"Sorry, Smash."

"Smashie doesn't like Patches a regular amount," said Billy. "But Mr Carper really hates him." He gulped and his face creased with anguish. "Didn't you see how he kept glaring at him and snarling at him and wouldn't let any of us near him? And even after he said we weren't allowed near Patches's cage, he kept making mean faces in Patches's direction. It was like he wanted to get rid of him right then! I couldn't leave the poor little guy in there with a creep like that. I didn't trust Mr Carper not to do something awful. When he said he had fed Patches after we came back from Mrs Armstrong's office—" Billy shook his head—"I didn't believe him. I hated the thought of Patches going hungry! And then I worried that if Mr Carper really did feed him—" Billy broke off, biting his lip. "I couldn't help but think that maybe he had *poisoned* him."

"Billy," Smashie said kindly, "I think you have let your imagination run away with you." It was nice to be the one saying that to someone else, rather than having it said to her.

"I think so, too," said Dontel.

"I know how it is," said Smashie. "Don't feel bad. I do it all the time."

Billy's eyes were haggard. He shook his head. "But Mr Carper really *is* awful," he said. "All he cares about is his hair!"

"Where is Patches now?'" asked Dontel.

"Behind the equipment bin outside the gym," Billy admitted. "I brought him back to school today. I was going to put him back in his cage, but then we had silent morning break again, and also Mr Carper keeps coming by our room—"

"I'll say," said Dontel.

"And I just couldn't take the chance." Billy gulped and lowered his eyes. "I was going to return him when the coast was clear – honest."

"I bet you hoped that everyone would be so happy

Patches was back that they would stop being mad at you, too," said Smashie.

Billy hesitated, then nodded. "It stinks when everybody is mad at you."

"We know," said Smashie sadly. "But it is no fun to be glued, either," she added, remembering how hard it had been to unstick Alonso.

Billy's shoulders sagged. "I've told you – that wasn't me," he said.

"Tchah," said Smashie.

"You don't have any proof it was him, Smash," said Dontel. "And I for one really don't think it was."

"Thank you," Billy said.

"No wonder you've looked so awful, Billy," said Dontel. "First people are angry because they think you are the gluer, and all the while you were worried about your plan for Patches. And then you had to worry about getting caught."

"Yes," said Billy. "I've been worried about Patches this whole entire time." He looked at them in despair. "Are you going to rat me out?"

"Heck," said Dontel. "It's not like you took Patches

for a bad reason. You were only trying to protect him. Right, Smashie?"

Billy looked at them hopefully. "Please, you guys. The kids'll hate me forever if they find out."

"You really love Patches, don't you?" Dontel asked.

"Yes," Billy said in a low voice. "Almost Too Much."

"What do you think, Smashie?"

Smashie stared across the lunchroom.

"There is more than one mystery afoot here is what I think," she said slowly.

"That's what I've been saying," said Dontel. "Two mysteries. The Patches mystery *and* the glue mystery. And now that we've solved the Patches mystery, we have to work on the glue one. I—"

But Smashie's gaze remained faraway. "No," she said. "That is not our priority." She stood up. "I am going to the staffroom this minute."

"Why?" asked Dontel.

"To ask Ms Early if I can convene a court of law in Room 11 after break!"

"A court of law?" Dontel was incredulous. Billy uttered a low cry and clutched his head. "Why?"

"Because stealing is *wrong,* of course!" Smashie cried, swinging her gaze to the boys at last. "People who steal ought to get their comeuppance!"

"Smashie!" cried Dontel.

"Come on!" said Smashie, grabbing up her lunch box. "There's no time to lose!"

Stunned, Dontel only shook his head.

"Fine!" cried Smashie. "If you don't care that two out of three mysteries are finally solved—"

"*Three* mysteries?" cried Dontel. "What do you mean, *three?*"

But Smashie was already gone, Billy's despondent sobs sounding behind her.

CHAPTER 25
Smashie Wants a Trial

Smashie sped around the corner and immediately met a little knot of adults heading her way. The group included Mrs Armstrong and a stout, older woman with an extremely complex hairdo, whom Smashie recognized as Mrs True, come to attend the TrueYum supermarket nutrition assembly scheduled for one o'clock.

"We are so grateful for your sponsorship of this assembly," Mrs Armstrong was saying to Mrs True as Smashie neared. "As you are the town's foremost woman of business, it means the world to have your imprimatur on our nutritional studies."

Mrs True smiled in a queenly way. "It is my pleasure," she said. "We at the TrueYum want only what is best for the kiddies."

"Too kind," murmured the knot of adults. "Too humble."

It would be terrible to get into trouble right now, Smashie thought, and forced herself to slow to a rapid walk, her arms and legs scissoring hectically toward the staffroom.

"I trust that the actors playing the Kumquat and the Honeydew Melon have arrived?" asked Mrs True as Smashie passed the group.

"Yes," Mrs Armstrong replied. "As has the entire troupe of Asparagus Dancers."

"Splendid."

Arriving at the staffroom at last, Smashie knocked loudly on the door and poured her wishes into Ms Early's wary ear.

"No," said Ms Early firmly. "After the accusations you made this morning, I'm not inclined to let you wreak more havoc in Room 11, Smashie."

"Please, Ms Early! Please!"

"I said no, Smashie. Who are you accusing now?"

"I will reveal all at the trial, Ms Early! I promise! I just know I am not making a mistake this time!"

"You thought you were right last time, too," Ms Early pointed out.

"Yes," Smashie admitted, "but—"

Ms Early held up a hand. "No," she said. "I'm sure you mean well, Smashie, but I will not risk more children having their feelings hurt. Room 11 is in enough upheaval as it is."

"That is why I want to do this! I want to un-upheaval us!"

"*No,*" said Ms Early again, her voice even more emphatic. "And let this be the end of it, Smashie. You don't want your classmates even angrier, do you?" With a warning look, Ms Early closed the door to the staffroom.

Smashie stared at the door, anguished. What could she do? Ms Early was resolute.

Smashie hung her head. Her heart was full of despair.

★ ★ ★

Smashie trailed behind the rest of her class as they filed back into Room 11 after lunch. Ms Early and Miss Dismont were at the front of the room, struggling to lift an enormous framed map of the world off the wall.

"Take your seats right away, class," Ms Early said, puffing.

"What are you doing, Ms Early?" asked Jacinda.

Ms Early eased her side of the map down. "I'm lending our map to Miss Dismont for her room's lesson on cartography," she explained. "She needs a good big one."

"It looks awfully heavy," said Alonso.

"It is," wheezed Miss Dismont.

"How *could* you—?" Dontel started to say as Smashie sagged into her seat, but Ms Early's voice interrupted him.

"Class, we are going to get right to work this afternoon." Ms Early's voice was firm.

Smashie opened her mouth. Ms Early gave her a sharp look.

Smashie closed her mouth.

Ms Early nodded. "I am going to help Miss

Dismont carry this map into her room," she said, "and I will be *right back*. In the meantime, I want all of you to take out your independent-reading books and start reading. Silently. To yourselves. With no conversation." She paused at the door and looked at Smashie. "At all."

Grr, thought Smashie.

"Can't I help carry the map?" Alonso begged.

"No, Alonso," said Ms Early. "This is a job for grown-ups."

"The thing is as heavy as a house," Miss Dismont agreed. "But thank you for offering."

"Rats," said Alonso, and the two women left the room.

Smashie's heart began to beat. Was this a chance? *But Ms Early said to read silently!*

What about justice, though? What was more important? Books? Or justice?

Both! thought Smashie in desperation. *But maybe right now justice is just the tiniest bit more important —*

She leaped up and made a beeline for the reading area.

"Smashie!" shouted Dontel as she sped past.

But Smashie paid him no heed. She flung off her Investigator visor and dug desperately through the pillows in the reading area.

"What are you *doing*?" cried Cyrus.

"Where is the white pillow?" Smashie shouted.

"Smashie," said Charlene, "we are supposed to be reading."

Dontel hurried back to the reading corner. Smashie looked at him with wild eyes. "Do you think this green pillow will do?"

"For what?" Dontel asked incredulously. He lowered his voice to a whisper. "To sock Billy with?"

Smashie stared at him. "No! For my Lawyer Suit! I can't be a lawyer without a poufy wig!"

"What are you two fighting about back there?" asked Jacinda.

"Yeah," said John. "What gives?"

Smashie whirled around to face Room 11. "An emergency is what gives!" she said. "I am about to conduct a trial!"

"A trial?" cried Alonso.

"What for?" John was suspicious.

Room 11 was all abuzz. From next door came the

thumps and bumps of the heavy map being levered onto a wall.

There wasn't much time to lose.

Smashie mashed the green pillow down on either side of her head. From the English crime dramas her grandmother and Dontel's watched together from the collection at the public library, Smashie had gotten the idea that all lawyers wore enormous wigs that made them look just like Bon Jovi, Smashie's mother's favourite Handel-haired rocker. But those wigs were always white.

"Green will have to do," she said to Dontel. "People will have to pretend it's white. I'll have to hold it on with one hand, though. Now I need a cloak!"

"Smashie," said Dontel, "are you sure about all this?"

"No," said Smashie. "I think green hair is all wrong. But I have no choice!"

"I mean about this court idea!"

"Of course I am! Aren't you? You need to put on a wig, too! We have to get started!"

"No," said Dontel. "I'm not putting on a wig."

Smashie stared at him.

The chattering of their classmates grew louder.

"Why is Smashie putting things on her head?"

"I think she knows something about Patches!"

"Where are my cupcakes?"

"Smashie, please!" Dontel's eyes were full of worry. "I know you don't like Patches, and Mr Carper is awful, but Billy—"

"Dontel," said Smashie, her eyes wide, "this is about justice. Don't you agree?"

"Is it really about justice, Smash? Are you sure you are not just doing this so that the kids aren't mad at *you* anymore?"

Smashie looked at him, aghast.

Dontel shook his head. "I'm going to sit down."

Smashie watched him go. Her heart sank.

Dontel did not agree with her. This was worse than when he didn't agree with her about hamsters. He was not going to run this trial with her. Smashie was all on her own.

Be strong, she told herself, blinking. *Stand up for what you know is right.*

Smashie drew herself up. Her hoodie on backward

because she hoped it looked more like a robe that way and her left hand holding the pillow in place on her head, Smashie stood before her classmates, looking, she hoped, every inch an English barrister.

"Let the trial begin!" she cried. The whole of Room 11 stared at her. "I've convened this court of law in order to reveal the identity of—" she broke off and looked meaningly around the room—"a criminal!"

Room 11 gasped. Dontel shook his head bleakly. More thumps and bashes came through the wall.

"Right here?"

"In Room 11?"

"Yes," said Smashie. "In our very midst."

"Is this to do with Patches, Smashie?" asked Charlene.

"Yes," said Smashie. "It is."

Room 11 gasped again.

"Don't get too excited, everybody," Willette warned.

"Yes, get excited! We *said* we were sorry, Willette," said Smashie. "Besides, this time I am completely positive – without a shadow of a doubt – about the

identity of a criminal mastermind who has been plaguing our school!"

"SMASHIE MCPEPPER!"

Smashie started. The thumps and bumps from next door had ceased, and the slightly mussed figures of Ms Early and Miss Dismont stood once more at the front of the room.

"What's going on here?" asked Ms Early sharply.

"Is that a pillow on your head, Smashie?" Miss Dismont asked, puzzled.

"You are all supposed to be reading!" said Ms Early. "I stepped out of the room for one minute to help my colleague and—"

"Smashie says she is doing a trial," Joyce interrupted her.

"What?" said Miss Dismont.

"Oh, no, she is not!" said Ms Early. "Smashie McPepper! I am ashamed of you!"

"No, Ms Early!" Cyrus's voice rose above the hubbub. "Let her! Please!"

"We want her to!"

"Let her do it, Ms Early!"

The class was fervent.

"We need to get to the bottom of things around here," said Alonso.

"Yes," said Joyce. "Room 11 is a mess. Maybe this can help."

"And if Smashie's wrong again, you can just punish her some more," Jacinda pointed out.

"Hey," said Smashie.

"I've a mind to do that anyway," said Ms Early.

"Let her do it, Ms Early," John cajoled. "Please. It's her own neck on the line, isn't it?"

Ms Early's eyes met Miss Dismont's. Then she sighed.

"I don't know what things have come to in our room," she said, "but I can see that none of you will be able to pay a bit of mind to your work if we don't get this sorted out. All right. I will let you proceed, Smashie. Against my better judgment, mind you, and with the caveat—"

Smashie made a mental note to add *caveat* to her list of Investigator Language.

"That if more harm than good comes of this, you will suffer the consequences."

"All right," said Smashie. "That's fair." *But I won't have to suffer any consequences,* she thought. *Because I know I am right this time!*

"May I watch, too?" asked Miss Dismont. "My children are in charge of cleaning the lunch tables, so I have a few minutes. This all sounds very intriguing."

"Why not," said Ms Early.

"I'd be very glad to have you, Miss Dismont," said Smashie earnestly. She turned back to the class. "Where was I?"

"'Criminal mastermind,'" said Charlene.

"Right," said Smashie. But before she could pick up the thread of her thoughts, the door to Room 11 was flung open yet again, and Mr Carper poked his head round. "Ugh!" Smashie cried.

"Ms Early?" Once again, Mr Carper froze when he saw the class. "Why are you kids always in here?" he asked.

"What can we do for you, Mr Carper?" asked Ms Early wearily. Miss Dismont grinned.

"I just unloaded those infants," Mr Carper told her, flashing a smile, "and I thought I'd come here and, um, wait for you. I thought maybe we could, oh, I don't know, head down to the nutrition assembly together?"

"The assembly doesn't start for another fifteen minutes," said Alonso.

"That's so," said Miss Dismont. "But why don't you join us in the meantime, Mr Carper?" And she beamed at Ms Early.

Ms Early gave her a long, level look. "Yes," she said. "Why don't you?"

"Really?" said Mr Carper, moving quickly to an empty chair beside Siggie. "Because that'd be great. I suppose you'll go a little early, get good seats and whatnot?"

"It's only about vegetables, Mr Carper," said Jacinda.

"And the chance of a lifetime, Girl with the Hair."

"What?"

"What did you call my student?"

"Never mind. What's going on in here, anyway?"

"What's going on here," said Smashie, "is me."

"Smash!" Dontel's voice was urgent. He glanced toward Billy, who was blinking very rapidly.

"Smashie," said Ms Early, "please just get on with it."

"Okay," said Smashie, and readjusted her pillow. "Pretend this cushion is white, you guys."

Then, pacing before her classmates, she began. "Yesterday was a very dark day in Room 11. It was a day of terrible events."

"I'll say," said Alonso.

"And one of them," Smashie continued, "was that our room lost a valuable friend."

"Patches?" asked Cyrus.

"Patches," said Smashie. "Everybody was upset."

"Not you—" said Joyce.

"Yes, me!" said Smashie. "I keep telling you! And that is why Dontel and I decided to investigate."

"Oh!" said Charlene. "So is that an Investigation Suit that you have on? Underneath whatever this new suit with the pillow is?"

"Yes," said Smashie. "It is."

The class nodded.

"Go on," said John.

"We didn't do so well with our investigating at first," Smashie admitted. "Until this morning, when we got to go on an errand to Mr Bloom's office." She stopped her pacing and faced her classmates. "While we were at Mr Bloom's, we found important evidence about Patches's disappearance."

"Don't I know it," said Willette. "I'm still waiting on those cupcakes, Smashie."

Smashie whirled round. It was hard to do one-handed, but she did it.

"They are in my lunch box. I will get them for you as soon as I am done, Willette! What you don't know," she said, addressing the whole group once more, "is what the evidence was. We saw shavings. And food. Lots of it, for hamsters. I saved some in my Investigator Suit hat and Dontel put some in his pockets. Room 11, every bit of the evidence Dontel and I found—" she held her classmates in her gaze— "showed us how extra nice Patches had been treated by the person who took him."

"What?"

"Huh?"

The class was humming with questions.

"Dontel," said Smashie. "Isn't that so?"

Dontel nodded and began to smile. Smashie's heart lifted. *See?* she thought. *I told you it was about justice!* Billy stared at his knees as if not daring to hope.

"Yes," said Dontel. "I can vouch for that completely. The person made very sure that Patches was happy."

"Exactly," said Smashie. "So that let us know that Patches was taken by a *very kind* person."

Billy looked up.

"A person who loved him," Smashie continued.

Billy swallowed.

"A person who wanted only the best for him. Who was only worried about Patches not being cared for properly yesterday."

"But whyever would someone worry about that, Smashie?" asked Ms Early.

"Yes," said Miss Dismont. "Don't you take turns in Room 11 being Hamster Monitor?"

"We do, Miss Dismont," said Smashie. "But the truth is, our whole class was forbidden to go near Patches's cage yesterday. Even the Hamster Monitor."

"That's true," muttered Siggie, glaring balefully at Mr Carper sitting beside him.

"Forbidden, Smashie?" Now it was Ms Early's turn to look puzzled.

"Yes," said Smashie. "Forbidden!"

Ms Early turned to Mr Carper. "Did you tell these children they couldn't go near their hamster?" she asked.

Mr Carper drew back and looked a bit hunted. "They carry germs," he said defensively.

"No, they don't," said Jacinda. "I asked my dad last night and he said no. He said maybe Patches would carry disease if we lived in medieval Europe and Patches was a creature of the wild, but a hamster wouldn't give us a modern stomach flu like we've had here at school. My dad said our hamster was perfectly hygienic, as long as everything was kept clean."

"I knew it!" said Charlene.

"Children," said Ms Early, "don't be rude." Still, she fixed Mr Carper with a look.

He swallowed. "Shouldn't you all be heading down to the assembly?" he asked.

"No," said Ms Early. "Not yet. Go on, please, Smashie."

"The person," Smashie continued, "this kind,

hamster-loving person, didn't trust that Patches had been fed properly, even though *someone* had said they had done it."

She glanced at Dontel. He was smiling at her. She smiled back.

"So this person – this good, true friend to Patches – decided that the only thing to do would be to take Patches home overnight, feed him, and bring him back when things were back to normal."

"You mean when Ms Early came back," said Cyrus.

"Yes," said Smashie.

"That makes sense," said John.

Mr Carper made as if to stand. "I should just—" he began.

"Please stay, Mr Carper," said Ms Early. "I'm interested to hear more about your day with my students."

Mr Carper sank creakily back down. The children glared at him even as they began to buzz with questions.

"But who was it, Smashie?"

"Yeah, who took Patches?"

"Who, you ask?" Smashie flung her non-pillow-holding hand into the air. "Who was our knight in shining cargo trousers? Room 11, it was none other than our own beloved Billy!"

She flung both hands toward Billy. The pillow fell off her head.

"Billy?" cried Alonso.

"Billy?" cried Charlene.

Billy stood, wan but brave.

"It was me," he said. "I'm sorry, everybody. I just thought—"

Willette stood up and picked her way across the room to Billy.

"Billy," she said, "Smashie is right. You are a hero." She flung her arms around him. "Thank you for stealing Patches!"

Billy burst into tears.

John reached over and patted his shoulder. "That's right, man," he said. "Let it all out."

Dontel beamed at Smashie. She beamed back.

The room filled with thankful murmurs, except, of course, from Mr Carper, who muttered, "He's not bringing that animal back in here now, is he?"

"Billy," said Ms Early, "you must have been very worried."

Billy nodded.

"I am so sorry you had to spend a day like that," Ms Early continued. "Your heart was in the right place. But couldn't you have found another solution? One that didn't make you resort to theft?"

"But how, Ms Early?" asked Smashie. "You weren't here. Even Miss Dismont wasn't here! And everybody was already mad because—" She stopped. She certainly did not want to rekindle the flames of Room 11's glue-anger. "What I mean is that he kind of had to do it, Ms Early."

"Well, I don't know about that one," said Ms Early.

But Smashie was already gearing herself back up.

"But Billy is not the criminal mastermind I was talking about earlier, Room 11!" she cried. "The theft of Patches is nothing compared to the other crime that took place yesterday!"

"You mean the glue, Smashie?" asked Joyce.

"No!" Smashie cried, pacing up and down once more. "I mean something far, far worse!"

CHAPTER 26

Another Crime

"What do you mean?"

"Another crime?"

"Worse?"

The class was beside itself once more. Dontel looked at Smashie, puzzled.

She felt the top of her head. "I need my wig before I can go on, Ms Early," said Smashie.

"Never mind," said Ms Early. "Your normal hair will do."

"But it is only brown!"

"I think maybe that's better than green. Get on with it, please, Smashie. What is this second terrible crime?"

Smashie resumed her pacing. "No, Ms Early," she said. "Not the second crime. The third."

"The third?" asked Charlene. "There was another one besides the glue and Patches getting stolen?"

"Yes," said Smashie. "And the third—"she wheeled around to face her class—"also involved Patches."

Room 11 gasped.

Smashie gestured to Patches's cage. "The third crime was tricky to discover, because of how we were forbidden to go by this cage the whole day."

"Indeed." Ms Early glanced at Mr Carper, but he did not notice. He had seized the moment for a bit of modeling practice and was hunched as if over a prime roast of beef, a plastic knife and fork held above it in attack position.

"Yes," said Smashie. "And that was true because Mr Carper—"

Mr Carper's head flew up. "What?" he said. "Did

you say Mrs True? Has she been asking for me? Is it time to go down to the auditorium?"

"No," said Smashie. "I'm only still talking about crime. I am almost done, though."

"Well, let's hurry up, Girl with the Messy Hair," said Mr Carper. "I've got things to get ready."

"My hair is only messy because I had my wig on before," said Smashie coldly. "Besides, I thought I was Girl with the Ears."

"Well, you're lucky today." Mr Carper shrugged. "The hair is worse."

"Mr Carper!" said Ms Early.

"What?" said Mr Carper.

"As I was saying," Smashie continued, "one of the reasons we didn't see much of Patches was that Mr Carper said we had to keep away, partly because he was punishing us and partly because he said the cage was so filthy. Well, it wasn't filthy. I don't like to go near it much, as you kids know, but even I could tell that Joyce had done a very nice job cleaning it the day before."

"Thank you," said Joyce.

"You are welcome," said Smashie. "It got me to thinking. I really like Ms Early a lot. And I felt really bad that she was sick yesterday."

"That's sweet of you, Smashie," said Ms Early.

"I am only part-way sweet, Ms Early," said Smashie. "You see, I have a pretty hard time with Patches."

"I'll say," said Willette.

"Willette," said John, "she is giving you cupcakes."

Casting a thankful look at him, Smashie went on. "And so even though I really care about Ms Early, I don't think I would be able to do something nice for her if it involved Patches. Even to make her feel better. I could never, for example, clean out Patches's cage. So I thought it was kind of strange this morning when Mr Carper volunteered to do that. Why would someone who thinks hamsters are germy bundles of yuckiness offer to do a job like that for our teacher?"

Charlene winced and glanced at the substitute. "Um, Smashie?" she said.

"Ms Early is a very wonderful woman," Jacinda said pointedly.

"Also pretty," Alonso added.

Miss Dismont laughed.

"Children —" said Ms Early.

"Well, it's true," said Cyrus. "We all could tell that he —"

"No!" said Smashie. "I mean, yes, Ms Early is terrific, but it still didn't make sense. Mr Carper kept coming back and coming back, even though he was supposed to be with the Infants. And even though Ms Early didn't seem all that —"

"Smashie," said John, "don't shame the man."

Smashie turned to Mr Carper. "We know that you didn't have such a good time with us yesterday, so we aren't the reason you came back so much, right?"

"I'll say," said Mr Carper.

"So how come you did?"

Mr Carper shrugged carelessly. "What can I say?" he said. "All the push-pull – the woman clearly finds me fascinating. I was throwing the poor thing a bone."

"Excuse me?" said Ms Early and Miss Dismont in unison.

But Smashie was shaking her head. "That's not it. First he offered to clean out the cage. Then he came by again and told her she looked sick and ought to go home. And he was always mad when the room was locked, and he was always mad that we were here."

"Who wouldn't be?" said Mr Carper. "Look, I have an assembly to go to. I'm going to —"

Dontel stood up. His eyes met Smashie's.

"I think you should hear Smashie out, Mr Carper."

"Yes," said Smashie. "You should. Room 11, I started thinking about why would someone want us all gone so much? Why would someone be so upset he couldn't get into our room? And why would that same person want us to stay away from Patches's cage so bad, even after Patches had disappeared, and why would he offer to clean it?"

"Because he likes Ms Early and wanted to look like a good guy?" Cyrus asked.

"No," said Smashie. "He was just pretending to like her. What he really wanted was access to the cage itself!"

"Why, Smashie?" asked Jacinda. "Is he getting a

gerbil or something for his own house and wanted to steal our cage to keep it in?"

"No," said Smashie. "But that is a good guess. The real reason, Room 11, is that the cage contains the evidence of his crime!"

"Hey!" shouted Mr Carper.

"What are you talking about, Smashie?" Ms Early cried.

"I am talking about *this!*" And Smashie strode quickly to the back of the room to Patches's cage.

"Get away from there!" Mr Carper yelled.

Be brave, Smashie McPepper! Smashie told herself. *There is no hamster in there to be afraid of.* And, taking a deep breath, Smashie flung up the latch to the cage and stuck her hand into the bed of wooden shavings.

Scrabble, scrabble, scrabble!

"Stop right now, Girl with the Crazy Outfit!" Mr Carper was in a frenzy.

"It is not an outfit, Mr Carper!" cried Smashie, wheeling round. "It is a suit! An Investigator Suit! And it helped me figure out that you are a thief!"

She drew her hand from Patches's cage and held aloft the object she had retrieved from beneath his shavings.

Miss Dismont's kangaroo pin!

CHAPTER 27

Miscreant Apprehended!

"I thought I lost that!" cried Miss Dismont.

"You didn't, Miss Dismont," said Smashie. "Mr Carper stole it!"

"You're crazy!" yelled Mr Carper.

"No, I'm not! He stole it when we were in Mrs Armstrong's office yesterday morning, Room 11, when she was questioning us about the glue."

"Yes!" said Dontel. "I get it all now! He was over by the cage when we came back – he must have just finished hiding it!"

"So that's why he jumped a mile when he saw us," said Jacinda. She and the rest of Room 11 turned accusing eyes on Mr Carper.

"I don't have to take this," he said. "I don't care if I never substitute in the Rebecca Lee Crumpler Primary School ever again!"

He leaped to his feet and made as if to move to the door, but only stood, red faced and wriggling furiously in place.

"I can't move!" he shouted. "I'm stuck! My shoes have been glued to the floor!"

At Ms Early's request, Smashie had gone to get Mrs Armstrong, who now stood in Room 11, looming over the dishonest substitute. Mrs True stood beside her.

"I'd've gotten away with it, too," Mr Carper snarled, "if it hadn't been for you kids and all your blasted *thinking*."

Ms Early's eyes flashed. "Smart, kind, *thinking* children are the best sort of children there are, Mr Carper, and luckily Room 11 is full of nothing but!"

"I second that," said Miss Dismont.

"Oh, Marlon," moaned Mrs True. "I never thought this would be the way we would be brought together! Why did you do it? Why?"

"It's all your fault, True," growled Mr Carper. "If you'd've just cast me in the circular last week when you saw me in the supermarket, I wouldn't have had to steal that stupid brooch to woo you with."

"*Woo* me? By stealing?" Mrs True pressed her hand to her chest. "For shame, Marlon! And believe me when I say that I would never let the face of a dishonest man represent the TrueYum!"

"For my part," said Mrs Armstrong, "I AM ILL IN THE HOSPITAL WITH A NURSE TAKING MY PULSE at the thought that such an awful person has been substituting in our school! I am taking this miscreant to my office at once to await the authorities."

"You can't," sneered Mr Carper. "I'm stuck."

"Remove your shoes. I shall take you in your socks."

"Room 11," said Mrs True as Mr Carper bent over his shoelaces, his teeth gnashing, "you have saved me from a nasty surprise. Thank you."

"Our pleasure," said Smashie.

"I speak for the whole of the TrueYum supermarket," said Mrs True, "when I say we would be honoured if Room 11 would star in our upcoming circular!"

"Us?"

"Yay!"

"We'd love to!"

Mr Carper stopped untying his shoes to throw back his head and howled, "Noooooo!"

"That is quite enough, Mr Carper," said Mrs Armstrong sternly. "Feet out. Come along."

And she led the wrathful sub out the door and down the hall, Mrs True following behind them.

It was much later. The TrueYum nutrition assembly was over. Smashie and Dontel had given Willette her cupcakes and she had waved them away from taking up her broom to do the sweeping. Mr Bloom had brought both Patches and the gluing materials back to Room 11. Now the class was using the final period of the day to process all the strange events that had happened. Miss Dismont had joined them, and as a special treat, Ms Early set Patches's cage on her desk so everyone could see him. Patches was darting about, settling back into his home.

Scrabble, scrabble, scrabble, went his paws.

"Isn't he the sweetest?" breathed Willette.

"He's the best and bravest hamster ever," John declared.

"Smashie," said Miss Dismont, "I still don't think I completely understand. I only lost my brooch this morning."

"No, Miss Dismont." Smashie shook her head. "You only discovered it was missing this morning is all. Mr Carper stole it yesterday, when you all were away on your field trip to the Natural History Museum."

"He must have hatched his plan to steal your brooch when he read the morning announcements and learned that Mrs True would be at the assembly," said Dontel. "When he realized that your class would be gone for the day, he knew the coast would be clear to steal it."

"He knew it would be the perfect wooing present for Mrs True." Joyce nodded.

"It really is beautiful," said Cyrus, glancing at the brooch pinned, once more, on Miss Dismont's shoulder. The class nodded in agreement.

"Dontel," said Smashie, "did you really think I was having a court just to rat out Billy?"

"I didn't know what to think," Dontel admitted. "It didn't seem like you to do like that, but you were so determined! I had no idea you were thinking about Mr Carper the whole time."

"It all happened so quickly," said Smashie. "I figured it out all at once, when we were talking to Billy. I guess I just thought you figured it out when I did. I couldn't understand why you seemed so disappointed in me. I am really sorry. I was too hectic. I should have slowed down and talked it all over with you."

"No, *I'm* sorry," said Dontel. "I should have known you would never do something so mean. I think you did a swell piece of thinking, Smashie. And I'd've done the same if I'd thought of it." He thought a minute. "Maybe not with a court of law, though," he said at last. "I think maybe I would just have explained things to Mrs Armstrong and let her come find the brooch."

"Hrrm," said Smashie.

"What I can't make sense of," said Ms Early, "aside from Mr Carper's decision to commit a crime, is why he hid the brooch in our cage to begin with. Why not just put it in his pocket?"

"It is a pretty big brooch, Ms Early," said Dontel. "And Mr Carper doesn't believe in keeping things in his pockets."

"He says it mars the line of the clothes," said Alonso.

"Well, I am very proud of all your smart thinking, Smashie and Dontel," said Ms Early. "You considered things carefully and well. And all in the name of justice! I couldn't be more pleased."

Take that, detective in Mrs Marquise's mystery story! Smashie thought, and she caught Dontel's eye and beamed.

"Me, either," said Charlene. "Thank you, Smashie."

"Yes," said John. "Put it here, Smashie." And he shook Smashie's hand.

"Thank you, John," she said, shaking back.

"I'm sorry I was so mad at you about Patches, Smashie," said Joyce. "Please forgive me?"

"I'm sorry, too!"

"And me!"

"And me!"

Smashie's heart bloomed. "Heck, it's okay," she said. "And I'm sorry I made you all feel bad about Patches, Room 11. I shouldn't have been so rude."

"Don't worry about it. You and Dontel are terrific!" And the class gathered around the two sleuths, slapping their backs and bathing them in thank-yous and smiles.

Basking in their classmates' appreciation, Smashie and Dontel looked shyly at their feet. The weight of the previous days' worries fell away from Smashie's shoulders at last.

"Smashie and Dontel weren't the only ones with great ideas today," Jacinda said with a smile. "That was some pretty quick thinking on your part, too, Billy. Not just about Patches. I mean gluing Mr Carper to the floor like that."

"It wasn't me," said Billy.

"Oh, come on. It's okay to confess. We aren't mad at you anymore."

But Billy shook his head. "It wasn't me, I tell you!"

"He's right." Siggie stood up. "It was me."

CHAPTER 28

Confession

"You're the gluer, Siggie?"

"You?"

"But why?"

"I don't rightly know," said Siggie. He twisted his
fingers and stared at the floor.

"I knew Billy wasn't the gluer," Dontel whispered
to Smashie.

"You *did*," Smashie replied, awed. "I am sorry,
Dontel. I shouldn't have been so quick to blame
him."

Joyce had overheard. "You knew, Dontel?" she asked. "Really?"

"Yes," Dontel admitted. "I did. And…" He glanced at Siggie. "I was pretty sure it was you, Siggie."

Siggie's jaw dropped. So did Smashie's.

Ms Early held up her hand. "We'll come back to that," she said. "But first, Siggie, I think you'd better explain."

"It all started in art," Siggie began. "I was using one of those little pots of glue on my project. You know – the kind with the brush attached to the lid. Brushing on the glue felt so smooth and gooshy and nice that I kept on doing it. I brushed glue across my ruler without even noticing I did it. I was just enjoying how it felt. Then I forgot to put the jar away when we were cleaning up. I only realized it when we were in line and about to go, so I just stuck it in my pocket. I was going to return it later. But then Mr Flake got stuck to the ruler and everyone thought it was Billy—" Siggie broke off, biting his lip.

"And you were kind of glad that everyone was mad at him," said Dontel.

Siggie nodded.

"But why?" asked Ms Early.

Siggie's eyes were downcast. "He plays a lot of jokes on people," he said finally. "And sometimes they're mean." He raised his eyes and looked steadily at Billy. "That tarantula in my work box was awful, Billy."

"I know," said Billy. "Sorry, Siggie. I guess I can see why you wanted to pay me back."

John shook his head. "That's not cool, Siggie. We're best friends and you let me blame Billy! After all I've done for you." He turned grave eyes to Billy. "Billy," he said, "I'm sorry I've been so hard on you."

"No sweat," said Billy. He was already looking happier and more rested than he had in days.

Siggie, on the other hand, looked ashamed. "Gosh, Billy, I'm sorry, too. It got out of hand," he said. "I'm sorry, John. For real."

"Hmmm," said John, looking darkly at his friend.

"But I don't get why you went on to glue Alonso," said Jacinda.

"That first time with Mr Flake gave me kind of a taste for it, I guess. And I had the glue right in my pocket." Siggie's lips curved, and then he burst out laughing. "I'm sorry," he gasped. "I'm just remembering how Alonso's hand looked—" He broke off, unable to speak for giggles.

"I know what you mean," said Billy. "Like when I think about John's pirate costume and the Halloween parade—" His eyes brightened and he began to beam.

"Don't do it, Billy," Dontel muttered, glancing at John's stormy face.

"Right," said Billy, and he stopped himself from laughing.

"Siggie," said Ms Early, "I am very disappointed in you. As a result of your actions, we are going to have to work hard to bring trust back into Room 11. I think you will owe the class a much more formal apology. And Mrs Armstrong and I will need to set some consequences for your behaviour."

Siggie nodded, eyes downcast, all traces of giggles gone. "I deserve them," he said. "I shouldn't've done it and let the whole class take the heat. I apologize, everyone."

"Hrmmm," said the class.

"On the other hand," said Ms Early, "I am very pleased that we were able to apprehend Mr Carper through Siggie's quick thinking this afternoon."

"Me too, Siggie," said Billy. "Otherwise, I bet the class would have thought I was the brooch thief as well."

"Nah," said Alonso. "Sometimes you are kind of a pain, but we know you are a good guy at heart."

"Thanks," said Billy.

"How did you guess it was Siggie, Dontel?" asked Charlene.

"After Smashie and I helped Alonso get his bala-clava hat off his hand, I remembered I saw a piece of fuzz fall off Siggie's hand when he came in from lunch," Dontel said. "So I picked it up and put it in my pocket. I don't really know why – I think I must have had some kind of hunch. And then today it came to me – the fuzz from Siggie's hand looked a lot like the fuzz we had scrubbed off Alonso yester-day. I was pretty sure it was a match and that Siggie had gotten the fuzz on his hand when he was sneak-ing the glue onto Alonso's hat." And he reached in his pocket and pulled out a tiny fluff of yarn.

"That's from my hat, all right," Alonso confirmed.

Siggie nodded, too, silent.

"Why didn't you say anything before, Dontel?"

asked Jacinda. "We had that awful indoor break!"

Dontel looked grave. "I didn't make the connection until much later. And I wanted to make sure I was being fair. I knew I needed to be scientific and compare the kinds of fuzz, and I didn't have an actual sample from Alonso's hat. With just my piece of fuzz I was afraid it was all just, just – what's that called, Ms Early?"

"Circumstantial evidence," Ms Early supplied.

Smashie was impressed. "That is wonderful Investigator Language, Ms Early!" she said. "I am going to add that to our list." She turned to Dontel. "But why didn't you say anything to me, at least? I would have helped!"

"Things were too crazy," said Dontel. "I only made the connection between the two kinds of fuzz while we were running back from Mr Bloom's office," said Dontel. "And I was more excited about investigating Willette at that point. And then we messed up so bad accusing Willette—" He glanced at Willette.

"Don't worry. We're good," she said.

Dontel continued. "I wanted to be extra sure. I didn't want to wreck someone else's reputation and make everyone even madder at me or Smashie. And then we were involved in making our cameras, and Smashie figured out about Billy, and everything heated up again pretty fast. There was no time to investigate about the hat, too. I'm sorry, Smash. I wanted to tell you."

"I wish you had," said Smashie, somewhat miffed. Then she remembered her own solitary thoughts about Mr Carper and smiled at him. "But I guess it makes us even."

Dontel grinned back. "I guess it does," he said.

"I'm glad I confessed," Siggie admitted. "It's bad, but it would have made me feel even worse if I hadn't and you guys did some kind of trial on me."

Ms Early sighed. "What a day," she said.

"Ms Early?" said Charlene. "May I please hold Patches?"

"Yes," said Ms Early. "You may."

Charlene opened the cage and took Patches in her cupped hands. She stood before the class. "Smashie and Dontel," she said, "Patches would like to thank you, too."

Smashie gulped.

"Come on, Smash," said Dontel. "Let's go up there."

"Won't you say hello to him, just this once, Smashie?" pleaded Willette.

Patches quivered.

"I will stay right beside you," said Dontel. "You don't have to touch the feet."

"Well," said Smashie. "I guess Patches *has* had a tough couple of days."

"Forced to conceal stolen goods and all," said Cyrus.

"More Investigator Language!" Smashie cried.

"And forced to *be* stolen goods, too," said Joyce.

"All right," said Smashie. "I will try."

Room 11 watched as she and Dontel made their way up and stood in front of the little hamster.

"He's not all that bad, right, Smashie?" asked Dontel.

Smashie looked at Patches. Still the same beady eyes. Still the same chicken feet.

Even so, she thought, *he is kind of brave*. It must

have been scary having Mr Carper snarling around and hiding pointy things near him. Not to mention spending hours in a yogurt pot.

Smashie extended a hesitant forefinger and stroked Patches, once, on the head.

"Yay!" shouted Room 11.

"You do love him!" squealed Jacinda.

Smashie opened her mouth, then caught Dontel's eye and shut it again.

"Well," she said, "I think what I do is respect him. And my grammy says that goes a long way."

Dontel grinned at her, and she beamed back.

"It surely does," said Ms Early. "All right, Room 11. Time to go home."

"We sure worked hard today," said Dontel as he and Smashie walked home from their bus stop. Some of Smashie's pouches had come off her macramé sash, but she didn't mind. They had served their purpose.

"We sure did," said Smashie. "We are a very excellent team."

"Slap my hand with your hand, Smash."

They slapped hands.

"Let's show our grandmas our Investigation Notebooks," said Smashie. "They will love our Investigator Language list."

INVESTIGATOR LANGUAGE
1. Suspect
2. Detective
3. Investigate
4. Motive
5. Exonerate
6. Access
7. Alibi
8. Perp
9. Tax someone with their crime
10. Caveat
11. Circumstantial evidence
12. Stolen goods

"Also how we figured everything out," Dontel agreed.

"Then we can staple together the pages of notes we took about this whole investigation and put them in a folder marked *Cases Solved!*"

"I like the sound of that," said Dontel.

"Homework tonight is using our pinhole cameras," said Smashie. "Want to do the picture taking together at my house?"

"Sure," said Dontel. "We can practice for the TrueYum circular."

"I know just what we can photograph," said Smashie.

"What?" said Dontel. "Our after-school snack?"

"No," said Smashie. "Us. With vegetables. In our Successful Investigator Suits."

"But we don't have Successf —"

"I know," said Smashie happily. "We will have to get to work."

And they did.

N. Griffin is the author of *The Whole Stupid Way We Are*, for which she was named one of *Publishers Weekly*'s Flying Start Authors of 2013.

Kate Hindley has illustrated many books for children, including *Worst in Show* by William Bee and *Don't Call Me Choochie Pooh* by Sean Taylor.